Praise for *Beyond Friendship: My Untold Love*

"In Beyond Friendship: My Untold Love, Shivam takes us on an emotional journey that resonates deeply with anyone who has experienced the complex dance between friendship and love. His heartfelt narration captures the innocence of youthful emotions while exploring the depths of longing and the challenges of unrequited feelings. With vivid descriptions and relatable characters, this story beautifully illustrates how love can blossom unexpectedly, leaving us both enchanted and heartbroken."

"Shivam's writing style is refreshingly candid, weaving Hindi and shayari seamlessly into the narrative, enhancing the cultural richness of the tale. The poignant moments shared between Shivam and Vanshika are both touching and relatable, making the reader yearn for their own 'Vanshika' while feeling the weight of the choices that define relationships."

"This book is not just a love story; it's a testament to the power of friendship, the pain of waiting, and the hope that love can bring. A must-read for anyone who believes that love often resides just beyond the boundaries of friendship."

"A beautifully crafted tale that speaks to the heart and soul. Beyond Friendship: My Untold Love is a journey worth taking, reminding us all that the path of love is often filled with unexpected twists and turns."

Beyond Frienship: My Untold Love

SHIVAM JAIN

Dedicated to the one who taught me the true meaning of love and longing.

Tere jaane ka asar kuch aisa hua mujh par,
Tujhe dhoondte dhoondte, maine khud ko paa liya...
Har pal teri yaadon mein khoya,
Bas tu hi hai, jo dil ko hai bhaya...

~Anonymous

The Call for Help

The afternoon sunlight slipped through my window, casting a warm glow that made everything feel calm and ordinary. I was lying on my bed, scrolling through my phone without much interest, when suddenly, the screen lit up with a call from **Harsh**.

Harsh has been my partner-in-crime since first grade. I still remember when we got caught sneaking sweets from the school canteen—just one of our many adventures. We'd been through so much together, from schoolyard fights over cricket games to hours spent talking about everything under the sun. The call from him felt familiar, like a little piece of our shared history flashing up on my phone screen.

I answered, expecting his usual energetic voice. *"Haan, bol bhai! Kya kar raha hai?"*

But his voice wasn't light-hearted this time. It had a tone of urgency, almost worry. *"Shivam, yaar, mujhe teri help chahiye,"* he said, pausing for a moment.

I immediately sat up, my focus shifting completely. *"Kya hua bhai? Sab theek toh hai?"* I asked, feeling a prickle of concern.

He hesitated before explaining. *"Yaar, ek problem ho gayi hai... Deepanshi ke saath."* Deepanshi was one of his close friends, though I hadn't met her before. He went on to tell me about how her ex-boyfriend had been bothering her, sending unwanted messages, and even showing up unannounced. *"Woh bahut zyada pareshaan ho rahi hai, aur mujhe laga tu kuch kar sakta hai,"* he finished.

There was no second thought in my mind. If it was for Harsh, I'd do anything. *"Uska number de, main baat karta hoon,"* I replied, my voice steady.

A few moments later, I had the guy's number. I took a deep breath before dialing, not sure how this conversation would go. The phone rang a few times before he picked up, his tone gruff and dismissive. *"Haan, kaun hai?"*

"Sun bhai," I started, keeping my voice calm but firm. *"Main Shivam bol raha hoon, Deepanshi ka dost. Woh tujhse baat nahi karna chahti, aur tu usko pareshaan kar raha hai. Yeh last warning hai. Samjhe?"*

There was a silence, then a scoff. *"Aur tu kaun hota hai beech mein bolne wala?"* he shot back.

I felt my patience slipping. *"Main woh hoon jo apni doston ke liye kuch bhi kar sakta hai,"* I replied, making my tone clear. *"Uske aas-paas bhi dikh mat jaana. Yeh last baar bol raha hoon."*

He muttered something under his breath before hanging up. I sighed, hoping this would be the end of it.

I texted Harsh quickly: **Bhai, baat ho gayi. Usko samjha diya.**

His reply came back within seconds: **Thank you, bhai. Bahut bada kaam kiya tune.**

The Group Chat Begins

Later that evening, my phone buzzed with a notification. Harsh had created an Instagram group chat titled *"Humari Gang"*. There were four members: **me**, **Harsh**, **Deepanshi**, and someone named **Vanshika**, who everyone referred to as *Vanshu*.

I greeted everyone in the group, and the messages started flowing. Harsh, being his usual self, was cracking jokes and keeping things lively. Deepanshi seemed quieter, her replies brief but friendly. But there was one person who caught my attention—*Vanshika*.

Vanshika's words had a rhythm to them, like a soft melody. Her calm presence in the chat felt as refreshing as the Himachali breeze she often described. There was a calmness to her that stood out, and I found myself rereading her words, curious about the person behind them. We exchanged a few words here and there, but something about her presence intrigued me.

I tried to ignore it, but her messages stayed in my mind long after our chat ended that night. And as I lay in bed, I caught myself wondering about her—who she was, what her story was, and why I felt this strange pull toward someone I'd just met.

The days that followed felt like a blur of messages. What started as a group for Deepanshi's support turned into something more—a small, cozy space where we'd all share jokes, updates, and random thoughts. Each new message felt like a small moment of warmth in my day.

Harsh, of course, was the loudest. He had this way of bringing everyone together, dragging us into debates over everything from cricket scores to the best late-night street food in Delhi. Deepanshi added her own quiet humor, balancing out his loud energy. And then there was *Vanshika*, or *Vanshu* as everyone called her.

Every time her name popped up on the screen, I'd find myself lingering on her messages a little longer. Her words were different—calm, simple, but thoughtful in a way that made them stand out. I didn't know what it was, but something about her pulled me in.

One evening, she shared a song in the chat, a classic Himachali tune. The melody had this softness, like a gentle reminder of mountains and rivers far away from the city noise.

"Yeh gaana suna hai tumne?" she asked, tagging everyone.

Harsh quickly responded with his usual humor, *"Arrey yaar, main toh Dilli wala banda hoon. Mountain music mere bass ki baat nahi."*

But I couldn't help myself. I replied, *"Suna hai... but aise gaane waise hi khaas lagte hain jab koi Himachali hi suggest kare."*

A moment later, Vanshika's reply appeared, *"Toh tumne uss jagah ki baat samajh li... not bad, Shivam."* She added a winking emoji, and for some reason, it made me smile.

As our conversations grew, I found myself looking forward to each notification, each little piece of her world that she shared. Her love for Himachal was deep, woven into the things she spoke about—the songs, the quiet places, and the memories she held close.

One night, after the group had gone quiet, I couldn't shake the feeling that something was beginning to shift inside me. It was like a quiet echo that grew a little louder every time I thought of her.

In the silence of my room, a line of shayari floated into my mind:

Mere dil mein ek ajeeb si hulchul si hai,
Jo tere khayalon ke saath aur bhi gehri ho jaati hai...

I wasn't sure what these feelings meant, or where they would lead. But as I drifted off to sleep that night, her messages lingered in my thoughts, a comforting presence that filled the spaces of my mind with something both familiar and unknown.

As the days rolled on, the group chat became my favorite part of each day. Every time I saw the notification, I'd smile a little, already anticipating Vanshika's messages. It was strange—I couldn't quite understand this pull I felt, but I knew one thing for sure: there was something about her that felt… different.

One evening, Harsh messaged me privately.
"Bhai, kya chal raha hai? Tum toh bade busy lagte ho Vanshika ke replies mein aajkal," he joked, adding a laughing emoji.

I quickly typed back, trying to keep things casual.
"Kuch nahi yaar, bas aise hi. Tujhe toh bas tease karna hai."

But he wasn't done. *"Accha, toh tu maanta hai kuch toh special hai na? Dekh, mujhe kuch toh shakk ho raha hai."*

My heart skipped a beat, but I tried to laugh it off. *"Kuch nahi bhai, bas dosti hai."*

Harsh didn't press any further, but his words stayed with me, leaving me slightly uneasy. I wasn't ready to admit my feelings—not even to myself—and yet, somehow, he'd managed to see through me.

Later that night, as I lay in bed, I found myself scrolling through our group chat, reading through Vanshika's old messages. Each word felt like a glimpse into her world, a small piece of her life that she'd shared without even realizing its impact on me.

Then, as if she'd sensed my thoughts, a private message from her appeared on my screen.

"Hey, tum soye nahi ab tak?" she wrote, adding a sleepy face emoji.

Smiling, I replied, *"Nahi, bas aise hi. Tum bhi jag rahi ho?"*

She responded quickly, *"Haan... bas kuch soch rahi thi. Kabhi kabhi raat ko neend nahi aati na?"*

"Bilkul," I replied, feeling a strange comfort in her words. *"Aisa lagta hai jaise saari baatein sirf raat mein hi sochi jaa sakti hain."*

She sent a laughing emoji, then wrote, *"Waise, Harsh ka mood aaj Deepanshi was one of his close friends, though I hadn't met her beforekuch zyada hi teasing lag raha tha."*

I paused, choosing my words carefully. *"Haan, woh toh bas mazaak karta hai. Tension mat lo."*

Her next message was simple, but it left me wondering if she'd noticed something too. *"Good... tumhe tension ho toh mujhe bhi ho jati hai."*

As I read her words, a warmth settled over me. I realized that even without saying much, we'd started sharing a connection, a quiet understanding that only the two of us felt. It was unspoken, hidden in simple conversations, but it was there—a small flame that grew stronger with every late-night message.

Before we finally said goodnight, I found myself typing out
a quick line, a piece of poetry that had floated into my
mind:

Tere khayalon mein jo sukoon milta hai,
Woh meri raaton ko aur bhi khoobsurat bana deta hai…

Her reply was just a heart emoji, but it carried a promise of
something deeper, like a small yet meaningful start.

As days passed, our interactions settled into a rhythm—an unspoken understanding between us. Mornings were filled with the usual rush, afternoons slipped by in classes and errands, but it was the nights that felt different now. Nighttime became our sanctuary—a time when the world faded away, leaving just us. when our group chat would fade, leaving just Vanshika and me lingering in our own world.

Our private conversations continued, each one more comfortable than the last. She'd tell me about her day, little things that only she seemed to notice. I'd listen, fascinated by her way of seeing the world, how she found beauty in things most people would overlook.

One night, she messaged me a little after midnight.
"Tumhe kabhi lagta hai ki kuch log bas aise hi special hote hain?"

I smiled, her words settling into my thoughts.
"Haan, lagta hai. Par kabhi kabhi woh log itne paas hote hain, aur fir bhi door lagte hain…"

She replied with a single heart emoji, and for a moment, I could almost feel her presence, like she was there beside me. It was a strange feeling—this closeness that grew through the distance of our screens.

But even as we grew closer, Harsh's curiosity about us didn't fade. During one of our group chats, he dropped another teasing comment.
"Arrey Shivam, tu aur Vanshu toh kaafi ghanti baja rahe ho aapas mein," he joked, adding a wink emoji.

I laughed it off, replying quickly, *"Bas tu kuch bhi mat soch. Dosti hai aur kuch nahi."*

But Harsh wasn't convinced, and I could feel his suspicion hanging in the air. Vanshika sent a laughing emoji in response, as if playing along with the joke, but I wondered if she felt the same tension I did.

Later that evening, after the group chat had quieted down, Vanshika sent me a private message.
"Harsh kaafi shakk kar raha hai tum par, lagta hai," she wrote with a laughing emoji.

I hesitated, then replied, *"Woh toh bas mazaak mein bolta hai, don't worry."*

But deep down, I could feel the weight of my own unspoken feelings. I knew that if Harsh kept pressing, sooner or later, I'd have to confront what was growing between me and Vanshika. For now, though, I was content to let things stay as they were, to keep our connection hidden in these quiet late-night conversations.

As we said goodnight, I found myself writing a quick line, unable to resist:

Teri khamoshi mein woh baat hai jo lafzon mein nahi,
Tere saath waqt ruk sa jata hai, jaise ye lamha kabhi
khatam na ho…

Her reply came almost instantly, a simple *"Goodnight, Shivam"* with a heart emoji, and it left me feeling that somehow, even without words, she understood.

As each day passed, I found myself thinking about Vanshika more than I realized. Our late-night chats had become a steady part of my routine, the kind of habit that brought both comfort and excitement. I'd look forward to her messages, the little details she'd share that felt like a peek into her world.

One evening, she messaged me a simple question that left me thinking long after I'd answered.

"Shivam, kabhi lagta hai kuch log humein woh nazariya dikhate hain jo khud pehle kabhi nahi dekha ho‹?"

I typed back, choosing my words carefully. *"Sometimes, yes. I think a few people are special like that, even if we can't put a label on it."*

Her reply was immediate, as if she'd been waiting for me to say something like that. *"Exactly. Some connections don't need explanations."*

Reading her message, I couldn't help but wonder if she sensed the same pull I felt. It was a feeling that lingered in the spaces between words, something quiet yet undeniably real. And I knew that one day soon, I'd have to let her know just how much she meant to me.

The more time I spent talking to Vanshika, the harder it became to keep my feelings hidden. Harsh's teasing didn't help; he'd noticed the way I smiled at my phone whenever her name appeared, and he never missed a chance to bring it up.

One afternoon, as we sat at a café, he gave me a sly grin. *"Bhai, kuch toh hai tere aur Vanshika ke beech mein, right?"*

I laughed, brushing it off like usual. *"Tu toh bas kuch bhi sochta hai, Harsh. She's just a close friend."*

He raised an eyebrow, giving me a knowing look. *"Accha? Bas friend? Mera intuition kuch aur hi kehta hai."*

I forced a smile, hoping he'd drop the subject. But his words left me with a quiet realization that maybe, I couldn't keep my feelings a secret forever. And as I left the café that evening, I knew that sooner or later, I'd have to tell Vanshika the truth.

Unseen Bonds

As the days passed, I found myself drawn to Vanshika in ways I hadn't expected. Our late-night chats had become my escape, moments when the world felt smaller, quieter—just the two of us talking about anything, everything, and sometimes even nothing at all. It was strange, how someone I'd only just met could feel so familiar.

One night, Vanshika sent me a message just after midnight. *"So rahe ho ya jag rahe ho?"*

I grinned, replying, *"Tum online ho toh so kaise sakta hoon?"*

Her reply came with a laughing emoji. *"Acha? Matlab ab tumhare neend ka bhi main reason hoon?"*

I paused, my fingers hovering over the keyboard, feeling an urge to say something honest. But I held back, replying instead with, *"Bas, tumhare saath baatein karne mein time ka pata nahi chalta."*

There was a pause, then her next message came through, *"Kabhi kabhi lagta hai jaise kuch log bas humare dil ke kareeb hote hain, bina kisi wajah ke."*

Her words made my heart skip a beat. *"Haan,"* I typed back, trying to keep my response casual. *"Shayad aise log humare apne hi hote hain, bas samay ke saath hum unhe pehchaan lete hain.”*

A heart emoji popped up on the screen, followed by her reply, *“Tum waise bohot samajhdaar ho Shivam. Pata nahi kyun, but baat tumse karke hamesha acha lagta hai.”*

Every conversation with Vanshika felt like a small moment of happiness that I’d carry with me through the day. There was something so natural, so easy about the way we connected, like we were two parts of the same story. Even the simplest messages felt like they held a kind of depth I couldn’t explain.

One night, she sent me a message, her words carrying a warmth that lingered.

“Goodnight, Shivam. Tum ho toh sab kuch thoda aur achha lagta hai.”

I typed back, my heart racing as I replied. *“Goodnight, Vanshu. Tumhari company mere liye bhi special hai.”*

Her response was a heart emoji, and somehow, that simple gesture made everything feel complete. I realized, as I stared at her message, that she’d become a part of my life I couldn’t imagine letting go of. And maybe, just maybe, I’d find a way to tell her that.

Each conversation with Vanshika felt like an open door to something deeper. She had this way of making even the simplest moments feel meaningful, like a quiet rhythm I'd started relying on. It wasn't just about the words—we'd built something that went beyond that.

One evening, as we exchanged our usual goodnights, she sent me a message that made me smile.

"Thanks for being you, Shivam. You make things feel lighter, you know?"

I replied, feeling a warmth in her words. *"Tumhare saath woh lightness aur bhi badh jaati hai, Vanshu. Bas aise hi hamesha contact mein rehna."*

Her response was a heart emoji, followed by the words, *"Always."*

As I closed our chat that night, I felt a quiet happiness settle over me. Even if we hadn't named our connection, I knew it was something rare, something worth holding onto. And as I drifted off to sleep, I knew that whatever we shared, it was real.

Our conversations were becoming the highlight of my day, each message from Vanshika like a breath of fresh air. There was something beautifully simple about the connection we shared—unspoken, steady, and real. It was the kind of closeness that I hadn't felt in a long time, like finding a piece of myself in someone else.

One evening, she sent me a message about her day. *"Aaj Mumma ne bohot daant lagayi mujhe, bas mood off ho gaya."*

I replied instantly, feeling a pang of protectiveness. *"Koi nahi, tumhari mood ko theek karne ke liye tumhare paas main hoon na."*

Her reply came with a laughing emoji. *"Haan, tumhare bina toh mera din incomplete lagta hai."* The words left me staring at the screen, my heart racing. Even though she didn't say it directly, there was something in those words that made me feel like maybe she felt the same way I did.

Our conversations would sometimes drift into the night, filled with light banter, memories, and even silence. But each pause felt comforting, like we were both simply… present.

The Push and Pull of Friendship

But even as our friendship deepened, I could feel the weight of my own unspoken feelings. I'd catch myself smiling at her messages, waiting for her replies like they held a piece of something precious. And each time I felt this way, I'd remind myself of the boundaries we'd set, unsure if I was willing to risk our friendship for something that may never happen.

One evening, I told Sujal, my best friend since seventh grade, about my growing connection with Vanshika. He listened, his tone serious but encouraging.

"Bhai, woh teri zindagi mein kuch khaas lagti hai," he said after a pause. *"Lekin agar tu khud ko sambhal nahi paaya toh shayad tu apni dosti bhi risk mein daal dega."*

His words made me pause. He was right; I had to be careful. But knowing that didn't change the way I felt, and that night, as I messaged Vanshika, I realized that she'd already become a part of my life I couldn't let go of.

We ended our conversation with a shayari she shared, one that echoed the way I felt:

Mere jazbaaton ki daastaan tujhe pati hai par tu jaanti nahi,
Tere khayalon mein main kho gaya hoon, aur tu mujhe samajh paati nahi...

I stared at her words, the shayari lingering in my thoughts long after we said goodnight. In her simplicity, she had managed to touch something deep within me, a feeling I didn't know how to put into words. It was a connection that went beyond friendship—a bond that I knew would stay with me, even if things didn't turn out as I hoped.

The more time I spent talking to Vanshu, the more I found myself slipping into a habit I couldn't break. Our messages had become a constant part of my day—each notification was like a small burst of excitement, a reminder that she was there, somewhere, sharing this strange journey with me.

One night, as we were chatting, she shared a memory from her childhood, a moment that had stayed with her for years. *"Woh ek baar main Himachal gayi thi, aur wahan ki shaam mein jo sukoon mila, woh aaj tak yaad hai mujhe."*

I imagined her as she spoke, her words painting a picture of mist-covered mountains and quiet, winding roads. There was something in her voice that night—a kind of longing that made me want to be there with her, sharing that peace. *"Kabhi phir se jaana hua toh mujhe saath le chalna,"* I typed back, half-joking, half-hoping.

She replied with a simple heart emoji and the words, *"Shayad... kabhi aisa ho bhi jaaye."*

The message stayed with me, a small promise hidden in those few words. Even if we hadn't confessed anything yet, even if it was just friendship for now, these moments held a different kind of meaning. It was as if we were building something together, one small piece at a time.

The Unexpected Call

One evening, as I was scrolling through our past messages, Harsh called out of the blue. His voice was light, filled with its usual energy, but his words carried a question that made my heart skip a beat.

"Bhai, tu aur Vanshu kaafi close lagte ho. Kahin mujhe kuch batane wala toh nahi?" he asked, his tone teasing but curious.

I tried to laugh it off. *"Arrey yaar, tu kyun kuch zyada soch raha hai? Bas dosti hai, kuch aur nahi."* But even as I said the words, I felt a twinge of guilt. Harsh had been there for me through everything, and hiding my feelings felt like betraying that bond.

Still, I wasn't ready to admit anything—not yet. I didn't know where things with Vanshika were headed, and I wanted to keep these feelings safe, like a quiet secret I wasn't ready to share.

Harsh laughed, brushing off his own suspicion, and we shifted the conversation to lighter topics. But his words lingered, a reminder that sooner or later, the truth would come out, and I'd have to confront what this connection with Vanshika truly meant.

Late-Night Reflections

That night, as I lay in bed, Vanshika sent me a message, her words simple but filled with a warmth that chased away the lingering tension.

"Tumhare bina yeh raat adhuri lagti hai. Thank you for being there, Shivam."

I read her words over and over, feeling a wave of emotion I hadn't expected. There was something in her message—a kind of trust that made me want to protect her, to be there no matter what happened.

As I replied, a line of shayari floated into my mind, capturing the quiet strength of our bond:

Tere saath ye raat mein ek ajeeb sukoon hai,
Jaise tum ho toh sab kuch apne aap sahi lagta hai...

Her reply was a soft *"Goodnight, Shivam,"* with a heart emoji, but somehow, it was enough. As I closed my eyes, I knew that whatever this was, I wasn't ready to let it go.

Every day felt like a quiet discovery. Vanshika and I hadn't spoken openly about our feelings, but there was an unspoken understanding—a comfort that needed no words. She was there, and I was there, and that was enough.

One evening, after a long day, she messaged me, her words carrying a familiar warmth.
"Tumhe pata hai, kabhi kabhi lagta hai jaise hum dono bas ek ajeeb sa connection share karte hain. Bina bole bhi sab kuch keh dete hain."

Her words felt like a mirror of my own feelings, like she'd put into words what I hadn't dared to say. I replied, trying to keep my response casual but heartfelt.
"Haan, kuch log toh aise hi hote hain na. Unke saath bas ek ajeeb sa sukoon hota hai."

A heart emoji appeared on the screen, and it made me smile, realizing how simple moments like these had become my favorite part of the day. Each message felt like a small, shared secret, a piece of something just between us.

Harsh's Growing Curiosity

But even as our connection deepened, Harsh's teasing became more frequent. He seemed to notice the quiet changes in me, the way I'd smile at my phone or the late-night texts I'd wait up for. He never said it outright, but I could feel his curiosity building.

One afternoon, Harsh messaged me privately. *"Bhai, tu aur Vanshu kuch zyada hi close ho gaye ho lagta hai. Kahin sach mein kuch toh nahi hai na?"*

I could feel my heart race as I typed back, trying to sound as casual as possible. *"Arrey yaar, bas woh aur main ache dost hain. Tu itna overthink mat kar."*

He replied with a laughing emoji but didn't push further. Still, I knew this wasn't the end. Harsh had a way of figuring things out, and I could only hope he wouldn't put the pieces together too soon.

Moments of Vulnerability

Later that night, as I lay in bed scrolling through our old messages, Vanshika sent me a late-night text. *"Shivam, kabhi lagta hai ki duniya mein bohot kuch complicated ho gaya hai?"*

Her words carried a heaviness, a kind of vulnerability that made me pause. *"Haan, kabhi kabhi lagta hai. Lekin agar sath mein koi ho jo samajhta hai, toh sab kuch asaan lagne lagta hai."*

She replied, *"Shayad tum woh insaan ho jo mujhe samajh leta hai."* The message was simple, but it left me with a strange sense of peace, a feeling that maybe I'd found something rare and beautiful.

I felt a wave of warmth wash over me as I typed back, unable to resist a line of shayari that captured everything I wanted to say:

*"Tere saath har raat khubsurat lagti hai,
Jaise tu hai toh koi bhi mushkil aasaan ho jaati hai…"*

She replied with a heart emoji, and somehow, it was all I needed to fall asleep that night, feeling as if, in that small message, we'd shared something real and lasting.

The days felt lighter somehow, as if every conversation with Vanshika added something new to my world. She was becoming someone I couldn't go a day without talking to, and I knew, deep down, that she felt the same way. There were no labels, no promises, just a connection that felt natural, like we'd known each other forever.

One evening, after everyone else in the group had gone offline, she messaged me privately.

"Aaj kuch ajeeb sa lag raha hai… jaise kuch missing hai."

I replied, smiling as I typed. *"Shayad tumhe neend ki kami lag rahi hai, thoda jaldi so jao."*

She sent a laughing emoji, then paused before replying, *"Nahi… woh sukoon lagta hai jo tumhare bina adhura sa hai."*

Reading her words, I felt my heart race, knowing that she was beginning to feel the same pull I did. *"Main hoon na,"* I typed back, keeping it simple but feeling the weight of the words. It felt like a promise.

The Strength of Silence

Even in silence, we'd started understanding each other,
filling the spaces between words with quiet meaning.
Sometimes, she'd send me a single message, something as
simple as "Goodnight, Shivam," but it felt like more—a
reminder that even on days when we didn't talk much, we
were still thinking of each other.

One night, I sent her a shayari, not expecting much in
return but wanting to share a piece of myself with her:

"Tere saath guzre hue har pal mein ek raaz hai,
Jaise tu mere dil ke kareeb hai, bina kisi awaz ke."

Her reply came with a heart emoji, and I could almost feel
her smile through the screen. There was a calmness in those
moments, a kind of peace I hadn't felt before. It was as if,
in this quiet space we'd built, everything felt right.

Harsh's Quiet Curiosity

But even as our bond grew stronger,, or the way my mood
would lighten every time I was talking to Vanshika. He
didn't say much, but I could see the questions in his eyes,
the way he'd sometimes pause, watching me with a slight
grin, as if he already knew.

One weekend, Harsh suggested we go out, just the two of us, for a break from the routine. *"Chal bhai, Adventure Island chalte hain, ekdum dhamal karenge,"* he said, nudging me with his usual energy.

The idea sounded great, a perfect distraction. But part of me felt uneasy, knowing that as long as I kept my phone close, there was a chance Harsh would pick up on something I wasn't ready to share.

A Hidden Crush

The weekend at Adventure Island was exactly the break Harsh and I needed. We'd been planning an outing for ages, and today, the energy felt right. The park was crowded, and Harsh was in his usual element, talking a mile a minute about which rides we'd try, his excitement contagious.

After a few hours of rushing from ride to ride, we stopped by the lake to catch our breath. Harsh, as always, was eager to capture the moment. He reached for my phone, his photographer instincts kicking in. *"Chal na, teri ek amazing picture leta hoon!"* he said with a grin.

Laughing, I handed him my phone. *"Theek hai bhai, bas photo achhi aani chahiye."*

He was moving around, trying different angles, when my phone buzzed with a message. I saw Harsh's gaze drift to the screen, and his expression shifted as he read out the notification under his breath.

"You're the best, Shivam. I don't know why, but I feel lucky to have you in my life."

For a moment, we both went quiet. I watched Harsh's expression as he handed the phone back to me, his face giving away nothing, though there was a faint smile at the corner of his mouth.

"Le bhai, hogayi teri photo," he said, sounding casual, but there was something else in his tone—like he'd picked up on something.

I took the phone, glancing at the message from Vanshika. My heart raced a bit, realizing how the words might've sounded to Harsh. I forced a laugh, hoping he'd think nothing of it. But the way he looked at me afterward, a hint of curiosity in his eyes, left me wondering if he knew more than he was letting on.

A Hint of Suspicion

Back at home that night, I couldn't shake off the feeling of Harsh's lingering look. He hadn't said anything directly, but the way he'd read that message out loud, the quiet smile—it was like he'd seen right through me.

For the next few days, things felt normal, but I noticed a slight change in the way he looked at me sometimes. I wanted to ask if he'd noticed something, but I wasn't ready to bring it up, especially since Vanshika and I hadn't even acknowledged our feelings yet.

As the days passed, I found myself drawn to Vanshika even more, her message echoing in my mind. It was as if, in her words, I'd found a reassurance I didn't know I needed—a reminder that maybe, just maybe, there was something special growing between us, even if we hadn't named it yet.

Over the next few days, things went back to normal on the surface. Harsh didn't mention anything about the message he'd read at Adventure Island, but I could feel a shift—a subtle curiosity that lingered in his eyes every time he saw me texting.

In our group chats, his teasing grew a bit bolder, each joke hinting at something more than friendship. I tried to ignore it, laughing along as though there was nothing to hide, but deep down, I knew he could sense something was different.

Late one evening, after the group chat had gone silent, Vanshika messaged me privately.

"Aaj kal Harsh ka mood bohot teasing lagta hai tumhare liye," she wrote, adding a laughing emoji. *"Kahin tumhe lekar kuch shakk toh nahi hai usko?"*

I paused, reading her message a few times, and then replied, *"Ho sakta hai, uska dimaag kabhi kabhi overactive ho jata hai."* I added a winking emoji, hoping to keep things light. *"Par tum tension mat lo, woh bas mazaak mein bolta hai."*

Her response was thoughtful, her words carrying a warmth that always felt reassuring. *"Good, kyunki tum par shakk ho toh mujhe bhi ajeeb lagta hai."*

There was a gentleness in her words, a quiet hint of possessiveness that made me feel something stronger, deeper. Even though we hadn't spoken openly about it, I could sense that she felt a connection too. Her messages held a kind of familiarity that went beyond friendship, a closeness that made every conversation feel more meaningful.

A Confession Waiting to Happen

One night, as we exchanged our usual late-night messages, I felt the weight of my feelings building up. There was so much I wanted to say, yet every time I thought of confessing, I'd pause, wondering if it would change things between us.

As if sensing my hesitation, Vanshika asked, *"Kabhi kisi ke saath aisa connection feel kiya hai, jo bina bole bhi sab kuch keh deta ho?"*

Her words took me by surprise. I felt a sudden rush of courage, a desire to finally tell her everything, to let her know that she was the one who made me feel that way. But instead, I replied carefully, unsure of her response. *"Haan, kabhi kabhi lagta hai. Par woh insaan kabhi saamne hoke bhi door sa lagta hai."*

She sent a shy smile emoji, then typed, *"Koi toh hoga tumhari life mein jo yeh feelings laata hai..."*

I could feel my heart pounding as I typed out my reply, feeling a strange sense of anticipation. *"Shayad ho. Par main uske bina bhi yeh sab nahi keh paata."*

There was a pause, and then she replied, *"Kabhi humare bhi waqt aayega shayad... jab dil ki baatein bina dare keh paayein."*

Her words hung in the air, filling me with a quiet kind of hope. It felt like a promise, a sign that maybe, just maybe, she was feeling the same way too. And in that moment, I knew that one day soon, I'd have to gather the courage to tell her the truth.

The more time I spent talking to Vanshika, the harder it became to hold back my feelings. Every message, every shared moment, felt like a thread pulling us closer, and I couldn't ignore the growing tension inside me. It was as if I was carrying this secret that could change everything, and yet, something kept holding me back.

One evening, she messaged me with a question that caught me off guard.
"Shivam, tumhare life mein kabhi aisa waqt aaya hai jab tumhe laga ho ke tumhe koi apne dil se samajhta hai?"

For a moment, I didn't know how to reply. It felt like she was asking me something deeper, as though she wanted to know if she was that person for me. I thought about typing out my feelings, of telling her that she was the only one who'd made me feel this way, but once again, I hesitated.

"Haan," I replied simply. *"Mujhe lagta hai ki kuch log humare dil ke kareeb hote hain, chahe hum unhe bata na paayein."*

Her response was immediate, almost as if she'd been waiting for my reply. *"Mujhe bhi aisa lagta hai… kuch logon ke saath kuch khaas rishta bas bante bante ban jaata hai, bina koi wajah ke."*

I stared at her words, feeling an ache in my chest. It was there, hidden between the lines—a feeling that neither of us had the courage to name, but it was real. The unspoken promise hung between us, a quiet understanding that made every conversation feel like a step closer to something more.

The Build-Up to the Confession

Our messages became more frequent, each one filled with hints that seemed to grow stronger. Even though we hadn't said anything directly, it was as if our conversations had started weaving a story of their own, one that neither of us could control.

One night, as we were talking about our dreams, she shared a piece of her heart, a vulnerability I hadn't seen before.

"Kabhi kabhi lagta hai jaise hum sab kuch keh nahi paate jo dil mein hota hai… jaise kuch baatein sirf samajhne ke liye hoti hain, kehne ke liye nahi," she wrote, her words lingering in the silence.

I felt a pang of recognition, knowing exactly what she meant. *"Haan, shayad kuch baatein bas dil mein hi rahe toh achha hai… kyunki kabhi unhe kehne ka waqt aur himmat nahi milti."*

Her response came with a heart emoji, simple yet filled with meaning. It was as if, in that small symbol, she'd told me everything I needed to know. I realized, in that quiet moment, that I was ready to tell her, to take the chance and let her know how much she meant to me.

A Moment of Courage

After days of gathering my thoughts, I finally decided to confess my feelings. It was late at night, the world outside was silent, and my heart was pounding with anticipation. I sent her a message, my hands trembling as I typed.

"Vanshu, mujhe tumse ek baat kehni hai. Shayad tum samajh bhi jao, shayad nahi bhi. Par yeh baat mere dil mein bhot dino se hai, aur main tumhe bina bataaye reh nahi paa raha hu."

There was a pause, and her typing dots appeared, then disappeared. I waited, feeling the weight of my own words settle over me, wondering if this would be the moment that changed everything.

"Haan, bolo," she replied, her words carrying a quiet patience that felt like an invitation.

Taking a deep breath, I typed the words that had been in my heart for so long. *"Tum wo insaan ho, Vanshu..... jo meri zindagi mein woh ehsaas laati hai jo bas tumhari wajah se possible hai. Tum mere dil ke sabse kareeb ho."*

Her response didn't come immediately. I could feel my heartbeat echoing in my ears as I waited, feeling the uncertainty settle over me. Then, finally, her message appeared.

"Ohh… Shivam, mujhe nahi pata tha."

Her words were gentle, not rejecting, but hesitant, as if she was processing her own feelings. And in that moment, I realized that no matter what her answer would be, telling her had been worth it.

There was a long pause after Vanshika's response, a silence that felt both full and empty. I read her words over and over, hoping for more, but knowing that she was just as uncertain as I was. Finally, another message from her appeared.

"Shivam, yeh baat tumne mujhse kahi, uske liye thank you. Par main tumhe kuch batana chahti hoon…"

I held my breath, feeling the anticipation building as I waited for her reply. Part of me already knew what she would say, but I wanted to hear it from her.

"Dekho, main kabhi kisi relationship mein interested nahi thi… aur yeh mere liye thoda mushkil hai. Tum jaante ho, main Krishna ji ki bhakt hoon, aur maine hamesha apne dil ko yeh hi samjhaya hai ki yeh sab mere liye nahi hai."

Her words were careful, gentle, as though she didn't want to hurt me. I took a deep breath, forcing myself to read between the lines, to see her honesty for what it was—a part of who she was, something she held close to her heart.

"Mujhe tumhari feelings ka bohot ehsaas hai, Shivam," she continued. *"Par main tumhe yeh waada nahi de sakti ki main is waqt is rishte ke liye ready hoon."*

I could feel a quiet ache settling in my chest, but I knew I had to respect her decision. I replied, choosing my words carefully. *"Koi baat nahi, Vanshu. Tumhare liye meri feelings badalengi nahi, aur main tumhari dosti se bohot khush hoon. Yeh sab bas tumhare saath share karna chahta tha."*

Her reply came almost instantly, her words a soft reassurance. *"Thank you for understanding, Shivam. Tum woh dost ho jo main kabhi khona nahi chahti."*

Reading her message, a strange sense of peace filled me. Even if things hadn't turned out the way I'd hoped, the connection we shared hadn't changed. It was still there, strong and real, something neither of us wanted to lose. And in that moment, I made a promise to myself—to keep this friendship close, to be there for her in whatever way she needed.

A New Understanding

Over the next few days, our conversations continued as usual, but there was a new depth to them, a quiet understanding that had settled between us. We hadn't crossed any boundaries, but the honesty we'd shared had left a mark, bringing us closer in ways that went beyond words.

Sometimes, she'd send me little notes of gratitude, things that would remind me of why I'd fallen for her in the first place.

"Shivam, tum ho toh lagta hai sab kuch theek hai... jaise tumhe mere saath hone ka ehsaas hamesha rehta hai," she wrote one evening, adding a shy smile emoji.

I smiled, replying simply, *"Tumhe bas yahi yaad rakhna hai. Main hamesha tumhare saath hoon."*

Her reply was a heart emoji, and somehow, it was enough. Even if things weren't the way I'd imagined, this friendship was something I treasured. And with every message, every small moment, I knew that my feelings for her would stay, patient and unwavering, as long as she needed.

Days slipped by with a new sense of understanding between Vanshika and me. She hadn't changed the way she talked to me, but there was a warmth in her words, an openness that made me feel like we'd both reached a deeper place. Even though she wasn't ready for a relationship, her presence felt closer than ever.

One evening, she messaged me with a line that made me laugh.
"You know, you're kinda like my personal therapist. Always there, always listening."

I chuckled, typing back. *"Therapist huh? Glad to be of service. Aur tumhare bhi saath ek free friend milta hai."*

"Free friend?" she replied, adding a laughing emoji. *"Then I'm lucky to have a therapist who doubles as my friend."*

Our chats were filled with a lightness that felt refreshing. Sometimes, we'd talk about random things—her favorite songs, old movies she'd watched a hundred times, or my latest pranks with Friends. It was like we were sharing pieces of our lives, building something steady and real without any expectations.

Comfort in the Small Moments

One night, she sent me a photo of her desk, cluttered with books and a cup of tea. *"Guess what I'm doing? Midnight study session."*

"Of course," I replied with a grin. *"You're the 'good student' type, aren't you?"*

She replied with a playful eye-roll emoji. *"Good student? Not really. I just panic two days before exams."*

I laughed, feeling the familiar pull in my chest that came with every message from her. There was something so simple, so comforting in these small exchanges, as if the more we talked, the more connected we became. I didn't need anything more; just knowing she was there, sharing these moments, was enough.

She sent another message, this one carrying a touch of vulnerability.
"Honestly, talking to you makes everything feel easier. Like I don't have to pretend, you know?"

"Same here," I replied, my heart softening. *"Bas tumhe yeh yaad rakhna hai ki no matter what, I'm here. Tumhare saath hamesha."*

A heart emoji popped up on the screen, followed by her reply, *"Thanks, Shivam. You have no idea how much that means to me."*

And with that simple message, I felt a quiet contentment settle over me, a reassurance that even without labels, we were something meaningful in each other's lives.

Every day, our connection grew a little stronger, our chats filled with stories, laughter, and little moments that became special simply because they were shared. She'd talk about her day, complain about assignments, or send me her favorite songs. Each message felt like a small treasure.

One night, Vanshika messaged me as I was getting ready to sleep.

"Guess what I saw today?"

"What?" I replied, curious.

"A random flower growing in the middle of the pavement. It looked so out of place, but it was beautiful," she wrote, adding a small picture of the delicate flower surrounded by concrete.

I stared at the image for a moment, a smile forming on my face. *"Only you would notice something like this. Tumhari duniya khoobsurat hai, I think."*

She sent a laughing emoji, then replied, *"Maybe. I just think the little things matter, you know?"*

"They do," I typed back, feeling a sense of calm as I read her words. *"Bas tumhari nazar mein hi woh khoobsurti hai jo baaki log nahi dekh paate."*

She replied with a shy smile emoji. *"Thanks. It's nice to share these things with someone who gets it."*

Shivam's Growing Feelings

As the days passed, I couldn't deny the pull I felt toward her. Her presence had become woven into my daily life, like a thread that kept everything connected. I found myself thinking about her at random moments, wondering what she'd think of certain songs or places I'd come across. And every time my phone buzzed with her name, my heart beat a little faster.

One afternoon, Harsh noticed my smile as I read one of her messages.
"Bhai, tu toh kuch zyada hi khush rehta hai aajkal. Yeh Vanshu ka effect lagta hai," he teased, nudging me.

I laughed, brushing it off. *"Arrey yaar, bas dosti hai. Tere imagination mein thoda zyada drama hai."*

He raised an eyebrow, giving me a knowing look. *"Tu jo keh raha hai, wo toh thik hai… par meri sixth sense kuch aur hi bolti hai."*

I rolled my eyes, trying to steer the conversation away, but deep down, I knew he wasn't completely wrong. There was something about Vanshika that made everything feel brighter, and the more time I spent with her, the more I realized how much she meant to me.

A Shared Secret

That night, as I lay in bed scrolling through our old chats, I felt a surge of gratitude. It wasn't just the words we exchanged, but the comfort and understanding she brought into my life. I found myself typing out a quick message before I could overthink it.

"You know, Vanshu, I feel like I've never met anyone like you."

Her reply came with a blushing emoji. *"Shivam, don't make me shy! But thanks, it really means a lot."*

I chuckled, then added, *"Bas sach bol raha hoon. Tumhare saath woh sukoon hai jo aur kahi nahi milta."*

She sent a heart emoji, followed by a message that made my chest tighten. *"You're really special too, Shivam. I feel lucky to have you in my life."*

As I read her words, I felt a strange warmth settle over me. Even without saying much, we'd found something rare, a quiet understanding that didn't need to be labeled. It was as if we'd built a world that was just for us—a world that felt like home.

Our connection grew stronger with every conversation, like a thread woven through my days, quietly holding everything together. I began to realize that Vanshika wasn't just a friend. She was someone who brought a sense of peace into my life, someone who made the world feel a little softer.

One evening, as I was walking home from a long day, Vanshika messaged me, and the exhaustion seemed to fade.

"Kaisa raha tumhara day?"

"Long and boring," I replied, smiling as I typed. *"Bas ab thoda better ho gaya hai, tumse baat karke."*

She replied with a laughing emoji. *"Tum bahut cheesy ho, you know that?"*

"Only for you," I typed back without thinking, then quickly added a winking emoji to keep it light. A part of me hoped she'd see the honesty hidden in my words, but I knew she wasn't expecting anything serious from me. And somehow, that was enough.

The Comfort of Knowing

Our chats became my escape, a place where I could share everything without holding back. She had this way of listening, of responding in a way that made me feel understood, even if I didn't have the right words. And I could tell that she felt the same—that somehow, we'd found a space where we could just be ourselves.

One night, she sent me a message that felt like a small confession.

"You know, Shivam, talking to you has become my favorite part of the day. It's like… you just get it, you know?"

I grinned, feeling a warmth spread through me as I typed back. *"I feel the same. Tumhare saath sab kuch thoda aur meaningful lagta hai."*

Her reply came with a heart emoji. *"Honestly, it feels like I've known you forever."*

Reading her words, I couldn't help but feel grateful. Our connection didn't need labels or definitions—it was something that existed in the space between words, a bond that went beyond what we could say.

Harsh's Curiosity Deepens

But even as I found peace in our friendship, Harsh's curiosity was never far behind. He'd catch me smiling at my phone or waiting for her messages, and each time, he'd give me that look—a raised eyebrow, a half-smile, like he was waiting for me to slip up.

One afternoon, we were hanging out at a cafe, and he finally brought it up.

"Bhai, tujhe lagta hai main kuch nahi samajhta?" he
teased, taking a sip of his coffee. *"Mujhe toh kuch zyada hi
lagta hai tum dono ke beech mein hai."*

I laughed, brushing it off as usual. *"Harsh, tu bas kuch bhi
sochta hai. Bas dost hai, yaar."*

He rolled his eyes, not buying it. *"Accha? Tum dono ke
chats mein 'sirf dosto' wali vibes toh nahi aati mujhe."*

I forced a laugh, hoping he'd let it go. But a part of me
knew he wasn't wrong. What I felt for Vanshika was more
than friendship, and hiding it was becoming harder with
every passing day. Yet, I wasn't ready to risk what we
had—this connection that had grown so naturally, so
quietly, that it felt like something I'd always had, even
before I'd known her.

A Silent Promise

That night, as I lay in bed, Vanshika sent me a message, her
words simple but filled with a warmth that chased away the
lingering tension from Harsh's questions.

*"Goodnight, Shivam. Talking to you always makes me feel
better."*

I read her message over and over, feeling a quiet sense of
happiness settle over me. I replied, choosing my words
carefully.

"Goodnight, Vanshu. Tumhe khush rakhna mere liye bhi zaroori ho gaya hai."

Her response was a shy smile emoji, and somehow, it was all I needed to fall asleep with a sense of peace. In that moment, I made a silent promise to myself—that no matter what happened, I'd always be there for her, even if it meant keeping my feelings hidden.

Our conversations had a rhythm now, a steady flow that made each day feel complete. Vanshika was there, in every moment that mattered, her words filling the quiet spaces I hadn't even known were empty. She'd become my go-to person for everything—the highs, the lows, and everything in between.

One night, she messaged me out of the blue, her words carrying a vulnerability she didn't usually show.

"You know, life feels so overwhelming sometimes. It's like... I don't even know what I'm doing."

I stared at her message, feeling the weight of her honesty. *"I get that,"* I replied gently. *"Bas yaad rakhna tum akeli nahi ho. I'm here, always."*

Her response came with a heart emoji. *"Thank you, Shivam. Honestly, you don't know how much it means to have someone like you in my life."*

I smiled, feeling an ache that was both sweet and painful, like a reminder that even if she didn't feel the same, our connection was something I could hold onto. And for now, that was enough.

Harsh's Endless Curiosity

Despite my efforts to keep things light, Harsh's questions never truly went away. He'd catch the smallest changes in my mood, the way my eyes would light up when I saw a message from her, or the smile I couldn't hide when I talked about her.

One day, he cornered me with a knowing grin, leaning in as if he'd finally solved a great mystery.

"Bhai, seriously? Ab tu mujhe sach sach nahi batayega kya?" he asked, raising an eyebrow. *"Tu aur vanshika bas dost ho? Mujhe nahi lagta."*

I tried to laugh it off, but his gaze stayed steady, challenging me to deny it again. I took a breath, feeling the familiar tension settle over me.

"Harsh, tune meri feelings pehle hi jaan li thi. Par humne kuch kaha nahi hai ab tak," I admitted quietly, hoping he'd understand. *"Woh aur main... bas yaar, main kuch risk nahi karna chahta. Uski dosti mere liye bahut zaroori hai."*

Harsh softened, his grin fading into a sympathetic smile. *"Samajhta hoon, bhai. Lekin kabhi kabhi toh lagta hai tum dono ke beech kuch aur bhi ho sakta hai."*

I forced a smile, knowing he wasn't wrong. There were times I'd catch myself imagining more—a future where things were different, where my feelings weren't hidden in silence. But reality was simpler. For now, we were just friends, and that had to be enough.

A Quiet Moment of Honesty

That night, Vanshika messaged me after our usual group chat ended. There was a familiar comfort in her words, a sense of ease that had become a part of my day.

"Thanks for always listening, Shivam. You're like my safe place."

I felt a surge of emotion, typing back with a gentle honesty. *"Tumhare saath bas yeh lagta hai ki sab kuch sahi hai. Like... I don't have to pretend to be anything else."*

Her reply came with a simple heart emoji, followed by the words, *"Same here. Tumhare bina toh kuch adhura sa lagta hai."*

I read her message a few times, feeling a warmth that settled quietly over me. Even if I couldn't tell her everything, knowing that I was important to her, that she felt a closeness she couldn't define—that was enough to make the silence worth it.

With a small smile, I replied, *"Goodnight, Vanshu. Tumhare saath yeh raat bhi kuch alag si lagti hai."*

Her final message for the night was simple, a line that carried a weight I hadn't expected.

"Goodnight, Shivam. You're one of a kind."

And with those words, I drifted off to sleep, holding on to the feeling that even if we didn't have a name for what we shared, it was something real, something worth waiting for.

Every message from Vanshika felt like a moment that belonged only to us, and as the days passed, I found myself drawn to her in ways I couldn't explain. We had our own world—a place where we'd share everything, from random thoughts to quiet, vulnerable moments. She'd become someone I couldn't imagine my day without, someone who'd made even the smallest things feel meaningful.

One evening, she sent me a picture of her terrace, the sky a soft blend of colors as the sun began to set.
"Just thought I'd share this. Isn't it beautiful?"

"It is," I replied, staring at the photo. *"But it's probably even better with you there."*

She replied with a shy smile emoji. *"You really know how to make someone feel special, Shivam."*

I paused, feeling a familiar ache in my chest, wanting to say more but holding back. *"Bas tumhare saath woh feeling naturally aati hai,"* I typed, adding a winking emoji to keep things light.

Her response was quick, and it felt like a quiet confession of its own. *"Thank you. Honestly, it's rare to find someone who makes you feel understood."*

Reading her words, I felt a surge of gratitude for every conversation, every shared moment. Even if we hadn't defined what we were, the closeness we shared was something I'd hold onto, a bond that didn't need labels to feel real.

Late-Night Conversations

As our conversations stretched into the night, I started noticing the small things that made her unique. She'd talk about her family, her dreams, and her love for simple joys—things like reading, watching the rain, or just listening to music alone. She had a way of seeing the world that felt so different, like she carried a sense of peace wherever she went.

One night, she messaged me about a song she'd been listening to, an old Hindi track that was close to her heart.

"Yeh gaana suna hai tumne? Kabhi kabhi lagta hai jaise purani cheezein bas hamesha se apni hoti hain," she wrote, attaching the link.

I clicked on the song, letting the music fill my room as I thought about her words. *"Tumhare saath woh purani cheezein aur bhi special ho jaati hain,"* I replied, feeling a sense of contentment settle over me.

Her response came with a simple heart emoji, and somehow, it was all I needed to know that she felt the same. There was an unspoken understanding between us, a quiet comfort that made even the silences feel meaningful.

Harsh's Gentle Push

But even as I cherished our bond, Harsh's questions
lingered in the background, a reminder of the feelings I
kept hidden. I could see the curiosity in his eyes, the way
he'd sometimes ask about Vanshika with that half-smile, as
if waiting for me to confess.

One evening, we were hanging out at a cafe, and he brought
it up again, his tone light but persistent.

"Toh bhai, kab tak ye 'dosti' wali kahani chalegi?" he
teased, raising an eyebrow. *"Kabhi toh dil ki baat samajh
hi jaayegi, right?"*

I laughed, brushing it off like always. *"Arrey, kuch nahi
yaar. Bas tu hi sochta hai zyada."*

He shook his head, giving me a look that was both
understanding and amused. *"Samajh gaya. Lekin kabhi
kabhi sochta hoon, agar tum dono ke beech kuch aur hota,
toh woh bhi acha hota."*

I smiled, feeling a pang of truth in his words. Sometimes,
I'd let myself imagine what it would be like if things were
different—if we didn't have to hold back, if we could just
be honest about what we felt. But reality was simpler,
quieter, and for now, that was all I could handle.

A Heartfelt Message

That night, as I lay in bed, I found myself typing out a message to Vanshika, letting my thoughts flow without overthinking.

"Thank you, Vanshu. You make everything feel so… easy."

Her response came with a heart emoji, followed by the words, *"Thank you for being you, Shivam. Bas tum ho toh lagta hai life mein thoda aur balance hai."*

I smiled, feeling a sense of calm wash over me. In that moment, I realized that even if we didn't say everything, we both knew how much this bond meant. And somehow, that was enough.

One evening, Vanshika messaged me after a long day. Her words, even in their simplicity, had this way of calming me, like a gentle reminder that someone understood, that someone was there.

"You know, Shivam, kuch log hote hain jo sab kuch itna simple bana dete hain. You're like that for me."

I smiled, her words making me feel seen in a way that was rare. *"Tumhare saath bhi woh clarity aati hai, Vanshu. Jaise tumhare bina kuch adhoora sa reh jata hai."*

She replied with a heart emoji, followed by, *"I'm lucky you're in my life."*

In that moment, I realized that what we shared went beyond simple labels. Vanshika was like an anchor in a world that often felt too uncertain, a reminder of something real and steady. And I knew that, even in silence, her presence was something I could count on.

Harsh's Quiet Realization

Harsh hadn't brought up his suspicions again, but I could sense that he understood something about me that I hadn't put into words. He'd see me scrolling through our chats, lost in thought, and give me a small smile—a knowing look that said he saw the depth of what I felt.

One night, as we walked home from a late class, he turned to me with a soft smile.

"Shivam, tu uske saath kuch khaas feel karta hai, hai na?"

I hesitated, then nodded, unable to deny it. *"Haan, kuch toh hai… par main apne aap ko rok raha hoon. Uski dosti mere liye bohot zaroori hai."*

He nodded, understanding. *"Kabhi kabhi, bas dosti bhi bohot hoti hai."*

And with those words, he dropped the subject, letting me keep my feelings to myself. It was a quiet moment of understanding between us, one that gave me a sense of peace as I continued to navigate my connection with Vanshika.

A Final Message for the Night

That night, Vanshika messaged me before bed, her words as familiar as a heartbeat.

"Goodnight, Shivam. Tum ho toh sab kuch thoda aur bright lagta hai."

I replied, a small smile playing on my lips as I typed. *"Goodnight, Vanshu. Tumhari baaton mein woh sukoon hai jo aur kahin nahi milta."*

Her response came with a simple heart emoji, and it felt like the perfect end to the day. In that moment, I knew that whatever this was, it was something real. Even if we hadn't given it a name, it was enough to make me feel grateful,

and as I closed my eyes, I felt a quiet happiness settle over
me.

The Confession and Hesitation

Days passed, but something had changed between Vanshika and me. It wasn't awkward or strained; in fact, it felt deeper, as though we'd both stepped into a place of honesty. I knew that she wasn't ready for a relationship, but somehow, being open with her had lifted a weight from my heart.

Our conversations continued, filled with the same laughter and warmth, but there was a quiet understanding now—a sense that we both knew how much we meant to each other.

One evening, as the sky began to darken, she sent me a message.

"You know, Shivam, it feels really good to talk to someone who just… gets it."

I smiled, typing back. *"Well, thank you for being that person for me too."*

She replied with a heart emoji, and it was like a promise—an unspoken agreement that we'd keep this bond as strong as it had always been.

A New Kind of Comfort

With time, I started noticing a shift in the way we talked. Vanshika seemed more open, sharing little things about herself that she'd kept close before. She'd tell me about her family, her dreams, and even her doubts. It was as if, in the space we'd created, she felt safe enough to let her guard down.

One night, she sent me a voice note of her humming along to an old song, her voice gentle and calming. Listening to it, I couldn't help but smile, feeling a warmth spread through me.

"Tumhari awaaz kitni sukoon deti hai," I messaged, hoping she understood the depth of those words.

Her reply was simple, almost shy. *"Thanks, Shivam. Kabhi kabhi lagta hai tum jaise doston ka hona hi kaafi hai."*

Reading her words, I felt a quiet satisfaction settle over me. Even if we weren't in a relationship, our bond was something rare, something that went beyond labels.

A Quiet Celebration of Friendship

The next weekend, I surprised her with a small gift—a book she'd mentioned wanting to read. I'd wrapped it in simple paper, including a note inside that read, *"For all the small moments that make life beautiful. Thank you for sharing them with me."*

When she received it, she messaged me with excitement. *"Shivam! This is so thoughtful. Honestly, I don't have words… thank you so much."*

I felt a sense of joy reading her message, glad that she appreciated the gesture. It wasn't about the gift itself, but what it represented—a token of the friendship we'd built, one that I knew I'd always cherish.

"Anything for you, Vanshu," I replied. *"Tumhari khushi mere liye bohot important hai."*

Her response was a heart emoji, followed by the words, *"I'm lucky to have you."*

Over time, the bond between Vanshika and me grew even more naturally, like a quiet rhythm that didn't need any words. She was there for me, not just as a friend, but as someone who genuinely cared. Our messages weren't just small talk anymore—they felt like conversations with depth, moments we both treasured.

One night, Vanshika messaged me unexpectedly. *"Shivam, have you ever wondered why some people just feel... different? Like they're meant to be in your life?"*

I smiled, typing back with honesty. *"Haan, lagta hai kabhi kabhi. Kuch log bas hamesha ke liye special hote hain, chahe hum unhe kya label dein."*

Her reply was thoughtful, her words carrying the same quiet warmth that had become familiar. *"I'm glad you're in my life, Shivam. You make everything feel lighter, you know?"*

I felt my heart skip a beat as I read her message, realizing how rare it was to find someone who saw the world the way I did. She had this way of making everything feel meaningful, like she noticed the little things no one else did.

"Well, the feeling's mutual, Vanshika," I replied, adding a heart emoji. *"I'm really grateful for you too."*

A Gesture of Care

One evening, she sent me a message saying she was feeling a bit under the weather. Concerned, I called her, and we spent the next few minutes just talking, me asking if she'd taken any medicine, and her laughing softly at my worry.

"You're such a worrywart," she said, her voice filled with amusement. *"I'm fine, really. Just a bit of a cold."*

"Well, take care of yourself," I replied, feeling a quiet satisfaction in being there for her. *"Aur haan, medicine zaroor le lena."*

The next day, I sent her a small care package with her favorite snacks and a handwritten note, wishing her a speedy recovery. When she received it, her message made me smile.

"Shivam! This was so sweet of you! Thank you. Seriously, you're the best."

I chuckled as I typed back. *"Anything to make you feel better, Vanshu. Tumhari smile meri liye bhot important hai."*

Her reply was simple, yet it held a kind of warmth that made everything feel right. *"You're too good to me, Shivam. Thank you."*

Moments That Matter

The days continued, each one bringing us closer, and it became clear that whatever we shared went beyond simple friendship. She wasn't just a part of my life; she was someone I wanted to be there for, someone whose happiness mattered as much as my own.

One night, as we wrapped up our usual chat, she sent me a message that made me pause.

"Goodnight, Shivam. You have no idea how much I appreciate you."

I smiled, feeling a sense of contentment settle over me. *"Goodnight, Vanshu. Bas yaad rakhna, main hamesha tumhare saath hoon."*

Her response was a heart emoji, and in that simple gesture, I felt the quiet reassurance that we both knew exactly where we stood. It didn't need a label; it was enough just knowing that she was there.

Days passed, and a quiet understanding settled between Vanshika and me. We'd both returned to our usual rhythm—our long conversations, the small exchanges that had become a part of each day. Yet, there was something different, an unspoken closeness that made even the simplest messages feel like they carried more weight.

One evening, as we were talking about random things, she sent me a photo of her bookshelf. It was filled with neatly arranged novels, each one looking like it held a story she'd lived through a hundred times.

"Tumhe pata hai?" she typed. *"Reading has always been my escape. Whenever things get too much, I just disappear into these books."*

I smiled, typing back. *"I get it. Tum kitabon mein woh sukoon dhoondti ho jo zindagi mein kabhi kabhi missing lagta hai."*

Her response came quickly. *"Exactly. Kabhi kabhi lagta hai books ke characters hamesha apne sath rehte hain."*

We fell into a conversation about our favorite novels, and for a while, it felt like there was no one else in the world. She had this way of making everything feel personal, as if she was letting me see a part of her she didn't show anyone else. And I realized, in that moment, that even if we weren't in a relationship, we'd built something rare, something that felt steady and real.

Vanshika's Subtle Affection

Over time, I started noticing the little things she'd do to show she cared—small gestures that made me feel like I was more than just a friend. She'd check in on me, remember tiny details I'd mentioned in passing, and even make sure I was taking care of myself on days when I was stressed.

One evening, after a particularly long day, I opened my chat to find a message from her.

"Hope you're okay, Shivam. Don't let the world drain you out."

Reading her words, I felt a warmth that was both comforting and bittersweet. I typed back, feeling the weight of my thoughts. *"Thanks, Vanshu. Tumhare saath sab kuch thoda easy lagta hai."*

Her reply was simple, but it held a kind of promise. *"I'm here. Hamesha."*

As I read her message, I felt a quiet happiness settle over me. It wasn't just about labels or expectations—knowing she was there, that she cared, was enough to make everything feel a little brighter.

As the days slipped by, I found a sense of calm in knowing that Vanshika and I had reached an unspoken understanding. Our conversations were back to their usual warmth, filled with laughter and small, thoughtful exchanges that had become the highlights of my day. Even though things hadn't changed in the way I'd initially hoped, there was a sense of relief in just being honest with her.

One evening, as we were chatting, she mentioned something that took me by surprise.

"You know, Shivam, I sometimes feel like I'm always holding back. Like I'm afraid of what people will think if I just let go."

I paused, rereading her message. *"I get that. Kabhi kabhi logon ke expectations hum par thoda bohot pressure dal deti hain."*

Her response came quickly, a quiet acknowledgment of something unspoken. *"Exactly. I don't know… it's just nice to talk to someone who understands."*

I smiled, typing back. *"Tum ho toh mere liye bhi yeh feelings samajhna easy lagta hai."*

It felt like we'd come full circle, that despite everything, we were still here—connected, close, and open. Our bond didn't need a label; it just needed the honesty we'd both shared. And in that moment, I realized that this friendship was more than enough, a foundation that I'd hold onto no matter what.

Small Gestures That Matter

Vanshika had a way of making even the simplest moments feel special. She'd remember little things about me, things I'd mentioned in passing, and bring them up as if they were important. It was in these small gestures that I saw her affection, even if it wasn't spoken out loud.

One night, she messaged me, reminding me of a story I'd told her weeks ago about my childhood.

"You mentioned how much you used to love riding your bike around the neighborhood as a kid. Do you still do that?"

I chuckled, surprised she'd remembered. *"Not as much these days, but those memories always make me smile."*

Her reply was thoughtful, her words carrying a warmth that felt like home. *"Well, maybe someday, you'll feel that joy again."*

I felt a quiet happiness settle over me, knowing that she'd remembered something so small, so personal. It was these little things that made me feel close to her, a reminder that even without promises, we'd created something meaningful.

Our connection settled into a comfortable rhythm. Vanshika's presence became a constant part of my day, her words and little check-ins forming the threads that held everything together. Even though we weren't "together" in the usual sense, she was the one person I found myself turning to, the one person who just… got it.

One night, she messaged me, her words reflecting the same kind of introspection that had been on my mind.

"Isn't it strange how some people just come into your life and make everything feel… easier?"

I smiled, reading her message over a few times. *"Haan, aise log kam hi milte hain jo bina kuch kahe bas sab kuch theek kar dete hain."*

Her reply was immediate. *"Well, I think you're one of those people for me."*

Reading her words, I felt a warmth spread through me, a quiet reassurance that, even if we didn't have a defined relationship, what we shared was real. It was a bond that didn't need explanations or promises—it just was. And somehow, that made it feel even stronger.

Small Joys and Unspoken Support

There were days when she'd message me just to share something small—an interesting quote she'd read, a picture of the sky at sunset, or a new song she'd discovered. It was as though we'd built our own world within these tiny moments, a place where everything felt a little bit lighter.

One evening, she sent me a line from a book she'd been reading: *"Sometimes, the heart understands things that the mind cannot put into words."*

I replied with a gentle acknowledgment, feeling the truth in her words. *"Maybe that's the best kind of understanding. When you just feel it, even if you don't say it."*

She replied with a heart emoji, and somehow, it was enough. It was in these unspoken moments that I felt closest to her, as though our silence held more meaning than any conversation ever could.

As the days turned into weeks, our bond became a part of my life in ways I hadn't expected. Vanshika wasn't just someone I talked to—she was someone who'd become my anchor, the one I turned to when things felt overwhelming or when I simply needed to feel understood. Even without any defined relationship, her presence was steady, unwavering.

One evening, I messaged her, just to share something that had been on my mind.

"You know, sometimes I wonder what life would be like if we hadn't met. Feels strange to think about."

She replied with a thoughtful message, her words carrying that familiar warmth. *"It would be a little less bright, I think. Some people come into your life for a reason."*

I smiled, feeling the truth in her words. *"Yeah, and they stay even without reasons sometimes."*

She sent back a blushing emoji, her reply simple yet meaningful. *"I'm glad you're here, Shivam. More than you know."*

Reading her words, I felt a quiet happiness settle over me. It was in these moments that I realized how much I cherished what we shared—the understanding, the simplicity, the feeling that we didn't need to be anything other than ourselves around each other.

The Joy in Ordinary Moments

Our connection felt like a constant rhythm, a quiet song that played in the background of my days. She'd message me with little updates about her day—how her classes had gone, or something her family had said at dinner, or even just a random thought that made her laugh. Each message was a reminder that we were part of each other's lives in ways that went beyond words.

One night, she sent me a picture of her study desk, cluttered with books, a mug of tea, and a small vase of fresh flowers.

"These flowers reminded me of you," she typed, adding a heart emoji. *"Thought I'd share a little brightness with you."*

I chuckled, feeling a warmth spread through me as I replied. *"Well, thank you for that. You're pretty good at making things feel brighter, you know."*

She replied with a simple heart emoji, and somehow, it was enough. In that small exchange, I felt the comfort of knowing that, even without labels, we were there for each other in ways that mattered.

Over time, I came to realize that what Vanshika and I shared was unlike any connection I'd known before. It was built on small, significant moments—those midnight conversations, her subtle gestures, and the way she always seemed to understand, even without words. There was a steadiness in her presence, a quiet comfort that made every day feel just a little easier.

One evening, she sent me a message that felt more personal than usual.

"You know, sometimes I feel like there's so much noise around us, like everyone expects us to be something… and it just gets tiring."

I read her message, understanding exactly what she meant. *"Yeah, kabhi kabhi aise log chahiye jo bas apna sath den, bina kisi expectations ke."*

Her response came quickly. *"And you're that person for me, Shivam. I feel like I can just be myself with you."*

I felt a quiet satisfaction reading her words. *"Same here, Vanshu. Tumhare saath woh sukoon milta hai jo aur kahi nahi milta."*

She replied with a shy smile emoji, followed by, *"Thank you for being here."*

In that moment, I knew that, even without defining what we had, our bond was something rare. It didn't matter if we weren't in a relationship; we had a closeness that felt steady, like something I could count on. And in a world filled with uncertainty, that was more valuable than anything.

An Unspoken Understanding

As our friendship deepened, I started noticing the little things she did to show she cared. She'd check in on me after a long day, remember tiny details about my family, and even share things with me that she didn't share with others. It was like we'd built our own language, a way of communicating that didn't need words.

One night, as we wrapped up a long chat, she sent me a message that lingered in my mind long after I'd read it.

"Goodnight, Shivam. I feel really lucky to have you in my life."

I typed back, feeling a warmth settle over me. *"Goodnight, Vanshu. Tum ho toh sab kuch thoda aur special lagta hai."*

Her reply was a heart emoji, simple yet filled with meaning. And as I closed our chat, I felt a quiet contentment settle over me. Even without promises or labels, we'd built something that mattered. And in a world where things were always changing, that was something I knew I'd always hold close.

Days passed, and our connection deepened in a way I hadn't anticipated. Vanshika was there, steady as ever, and each conversation brought a new layer to our friendship. It was a strange, beautiful feeling—knowing that someone was such a significant part of my life without needing a label. We didn't discuss my confession again, but something in our bond felt richer, more meaningful.

One evening, she sent me a message as I was winding down for the night.

"It's funny how some people can just… make life feel lighter, you know? I'm glad you're that person for me."

I smiled, her words lingering in my mind. *"Tumhare saath bhi woh feeling hai, Vanshu. Jaise tumhare bina kuch missing hota."*

Her response was a shy smile emoji, followed by a short line that seemed to carry more meaning than she probably intended. *"I'm glad you're here."*

I read her message a few times, feeling a warmth that settled in my chest. There was a subtle closeness between us, a familiarity that made me feel like I didn't need to say everything out loud. She understood, somehow, and that was enough.

Finding Joy in Simple Moments

There were moments when she'd surprise me with her thoughtfulness. She'd remember the tiniest things I'd mentioned—like my favorite tea or the fact that I loved old songs—and bring them up in our conversations. Each time, it made me realize how much she cared, even if we never spoke about it directly.

One day, she sent me a song she'd been listening to, an old Hindi classic with a gentle, soothing melody.

"This reminded me of you," she typed, adding a heart emoji. *"Thought you'd like it."*

I smiled, listening to the song as her words played over in my mind. It was a small gesture, but it felt like so much more—a quiet reassurance that she thought of me just as I thought of her.

"Thank you, Vanshika," I replied, feeling the words fall short of everything I wanted to say. *"You know me too well."*

Her response came with a blushing emoji. *"Bas tum ho toh yeh sab yaad rahta hai."*

Reading her message, I felt a quiet happiness settle over me, a reminder that even in this undefined space, we'd created something special—something I knew I'd hold onto, no matter where life took us.

As days went by, Shivam found himself drifting deeper into thoughts of Vanshika. Their late-night conversations were now a steady part of his life, something he looked forward to with a mix of excitement and calm. Every time her name appeared on his phone screen, he felt an unmistakable rush, as if he were seeing her for the first time.

One evening, as they chatted, Vanshika mentioned a small detail about her day that lingered with him long after. She spoke of the quiet joy she found in listening to an old Himachali song her mother used to play, a song that made her feel connected to her roots. Shivam listened intently, letting her voice carry him to the world she described, a world filled with mountains, rivers, and a deep-rooted culture he barely knew.

"Shivam, tumhe pata hai, wo gaana sunke aisa lagta hai jaise main wapas bachpan mein hoon," she shared, her words carrying a sense of nostalgia that Shivam found incredibly endearing.

"Bachpan ki yaadein hi kuch aur hoti hain, Vanshu," he replied softly, his heart warming to the trust she was placing in him. It felt like every conversation peeled back another layer of her life, bringing him closer to understanding her in ways he hadn't expected.

They continued talking, sharing stories that seemed inconsequential but carried a quiet significance. Shivam spoke of his own memories, of the simple joys and mischiefs he'd shared with his sisters, and of the little rituals that defined his childhood. With every word, he felt himself becoming more vulnerable, opening up parts of himself he hadn't shared with anyone else.

Late into the night, as they finally said their goodnights, Vanshika sent him a message that lingered in his mind long after he'd read it:

"Tumhare bina yeh raat adhoori lagti hai. Thank you for being there, Shivam."

Shivam's heart skipped a beat, his mind replaying the words over and over. There was something incredibly tender about her message, something that hinted at feelings she wasn't yet ready to admit, but he could sense them in every word. For the first time, he felt a quiet, hopeful confidence growing within him.

Growing Closer and Unspoken Bond

Each day seemed to bring Shivam and Vanshika closer in ways that words couldn't fully capture. Their conversations were no longer just about casual topics; they had become a space where they shared pieces of themselves they hadn't revealed to anyone else.

One evening, as Shivam reminded her about her medicine, Vanshika's response carried a warmth he hadn't expected.

"Thank you, Shivam," she wrote, adding a small heart emoji, something she rarely used. *"Tumhari yaad bilkul ghanti jaisi hai... bina bhule yaad dila hi dete ho mujhe."*

He chuckled, feeling a rush of contentment at her words. *"Bas ye samajh lo, tumhara reminder ban gaya hoon,"* he replied, imagining her smile as she read the message.

Their chats had developed a rhythm, a comfort that felt like home. Shivam found himself looking forward to her every text, each message feeling like a glimpse into her world. She had a way of making even the smallest details feel meaningful, whether it was the ritual of "Radhe Radhe" before sleep or the simple stories she shared about her day.

One night, Vanshika opened up about a childhood memory that left Shivam feeling like he was holding a part of her heart. She told him about her family's tradition of listening to Himachali folk songs on special occasions, her voice carrying a nostalgic warmth.

"Woh gaane mere liye sirf sur aur shabd nahi hain, Shivam," she admitted softly, as if sharing a secret. *"Woh meri bachpan ki yaadein hain… woh purane dino ka sukoon hai."*

Shivam's reply came with equal softness. *"Tumne kabhi sunaaye nahi woh gaane, Vanshu. Kabhi sunna zaroor."*

"Pakka. Tumhare liye zaroor sunaaungi," she promised, her words feeling like a gift he was waiting to unwrap.

In those moments, Shivam felt as though he were seeing Vanshika in her truest form. She was like a melody that lingered long after it ended, carrying a depth that he wanted to understand, piece by piece. And he sensed that, just maybe, she felt something similar about him.

As their connection deepened, Shivam began to notice the little things that made Vanshika unique. There was an easy grace in the way she shared her stories, her laughter filled with unguarded joy, and her words carrying a warmth that made him feel at home. She would talk about her favorite songs, her mother's wisdom, and the cherished traditions that shaped her.

One evening, their conversation took a gentle turn as they began discussing the pressures they each faced. Vanshika opened up about her family's expectations, the unspoken responsibilities that sometimes felt like weights on her shoulders. She spoke about wanting to meet those expectations while still staying true to herself.

"Shivam, kabhi kabhi lagta hai meri zindagi sirf meri nahi hai," she admitted, her vulnerability surprising him. *"Mujhe lagta hai ke jo bhi main kar rahi hoon, wo bas apne parivaar ke liye hi kar rahi hoon."*

Shivam took a moment, searching for the right words to respond. *"Vanshu, tumhe khud ke liye bhi jeene ka haq hai. Tum woh sab kuch deserve karti ho jo tumhe khush rakhe, chahe wo choti si khushi kyun na ho."*

Her reply was quiet, but he could feel the sincerity in her words. *"Thank you, Shivam. Tum hamesha meri baaton ko itne ache se samajhte ho."*

They fell into a comfortable silence, the kind that didn't need to be filled with words. Shivam felt as if he'd been given a glimpse into a part of her heart that she rarely shared with anyone else. In that moment, he knew their bond was something real, something beyond simple friendship. It was a connection that lingered, even after their words had faded into the silence of the night.

As they said goodnight, Vanshika sent one last message:

"Goodnight, Shivam. Radhe Radhe."

Looking at her words, Shivam felt a quiet contentment wash over him. There was a sweetness in the simple exchange, a feeling of peace that seemed to settle deep within him. He replied with his own *"Radhe Radhe,"* and as he drifted off to sleep, he couldn't help but feel grateful for her presence in his life.

As the days turned into weeks, Shivam and Vanshika's bond continued to grow, each moment adding another thread to the unspoken connection between them. They had developed a routine, a rhythm that seemed as natural as breathing. Their conversations often lasted late into the night, and even the simplest messages carried a weight that neither could fully explain.

One evening, as they were talking, Shivam noticed a slight change in Vanshika's tone. Her words seemed a bit more hesitant, as if something was on her mind but she wasn't sure how to say it.

"Kya hua, Vanshu?" he typed, feeling a tinge of worry. *"Kuch baat hai jo tum share karna chahti ho?"*

She took a moment before responding. *"Shivam, tumhe kabhi lagta hai ki hum log kabhi bhi apne asli emotions ko fully nahi express kar paate?"*

Her question caught him off guard, but he could sense the sincerity in it. He thought for a moment before replying. *"Haan, kabhi kabhi lagta hai ki kuch cheezein kehne se zyada mehsoos ki jaati hain. Shayad kuch baatein sirf ehsaas mein hi reh jaayein, aur woh bhi apne aap mein khoobsurat hai."*

They fell into a comfortable silence, both of them letting his words sink in. It was as if they had come to a mutual understanding—that there were feelings neither of them needed to spell out. It was enough that they both felt them.

Then, in an unexpected shift, Vanshika changed the topic, bringing up one of her favorite songs. She shared the lyrics with Shivam, explaining how each line reminded her of something beautiful and timeless. He listened intently, letting her words wash over him, feeling as though he were learning something new about her with every sentence.

"Tumhe Himachali songs pasand hain, na?" he asked, curious about her love for her culture.

"Haan," she replied, her tone softening with fondness. *"Woh gaane mere bachpan ka hissa hain. Unmein ek alag hi apnapan hai."*

Shivam felt himself drawn deeper into her world. Vanshika's connection to her roots, her attachment to family traditions, and her love for simple joys made him admire her even more. He realized that she wasn't just someone he enjoyed talking to; she was someone he deeply respected, someone who brought a richness to his life that he hadn't known he was missing.

Their conversation continued, flowing effortlessly from topic to topic. And as the night wore on, Shivam found himself wishing that these moments would never end. There was a peace, a quiet contentment in simply being with her, even through a phone screen.

As they finally said their goodnights, Shivam sent her a message that felt truer than anything he'd ever said:

"Tum mere liye kuch khaas ho, Vanshu. Goodnight and Radhe Radhe."

She replied almost instantly, *"Goodnight, Shivu. Radhe Radhe."*

And in that exchange, Shivam felt a warmth settle in his heart. He knew that whatever this was between them—friendship, affection, something unspoken—it was something he cherished more deeply than he could put into words.

The following days felt like a gentle dance between familiarity and mystery. Every conversation with Vanshika seemed to uncover something new, yet Shivam felt as if there was still so much left unsaid. They'd settled into a comforting rhythm, sharing bits of their day, sending random songs or quotes that reminded them of each other, and finding joy in the little rituals they'd built.

One evening, as they exchanged voice notes, Vanshika surprised him with a recording of her singing an old Himachali song. Her voice was soft, carrying a hint of shyness, but there was an honesty in her notes that captivated him. Shivam listened to the recording, letting the warmth of her voice wash over him.

"Tumhara gaana sunke aisa laga jaise main wahan hoon, un pahadon ke beech," he replied, feeling an indescribable sense of connection.

"Main bas yahi chahungi ki tum woh khubsurati mehsoos kar pao, jo mere liye un gaano mein hai," Vanshika responded, her voice filled with sincerity.

Their conversations had taken on a deeper tone. Shivam sensed that they were moving beyond the surface level, each willing to open up in ways they hadn't before. Vanshika shared more of her thoughts, her dreams, and the little things that brought her peace. And Shivam, in turn, found himself sharing stories he hadn't told anyone, memories he'd always kept close.

There was an unspoken understanding between them now, one that didn't require words to be felt. It was a sense of comfort, of being known and accepted without conditions. Shivam couldn't remember the last time he'd felt this way about anyone.

One night, Vanshika sent him a message that stayed with him long after he read it.

"Shivam, tumhe pata hai, tumhare saath jo bhi waqt guzar raha hai, woh mujhe bahut khas lagta hai."

Shivam's heart swelled at her words. There was a simplicity in her message, but it carried a depth that spoke volumes. He typed back, choosing his words carefully.

"Tum mere liye bhi kuch aise hi ho, Vanshu. Yeh ehsaas alag hai, par khoobsurat hai."

For the first time, he felt as though they both acknowledged the connection between them without actually naming it. It was there, a quiet understanding that lingered in every word, every silence, and every exchange.

As he lay in bed that night, Shivam realized just how much he treasured Vanshika's presence in his life. She had become more than a friend; she was someone who brought warmth, understanding, and a sense of belonging he hadn't even known he was missing.

Their friendship deepened with every passing day, becoming a steady presence in Shivam's life. The simplest moments, the little conversations, seemed to carry more weight now. Shivam found himself holding on to every message, every voice note, as if each one were a piece of something precious.

One evening, as they exchanged messages, Vanshika responded to one of his stories with a lighthearted comment, calling him *"Shivu"* for the very first time. Shivam's heart skipped a beat, an unexpected thrill spreading through him at the sound of the nickname she'd chosen. It was such a small detail, yet it felt incredibly personal, like she was letting him into her world in a new way.

"Shivu," he whispered to himself, savoring it, feeling a quiet happiness wash over him. That simple name, spoken by her, seemed to hold an intimacy he hadn't felt before. It was as if she'd given him a piece of her own affection, something that was just theirs.

He typed back with a smile, unable to resist teasing her a bit. *"Vanshu, tumhe shayad pata bhi nahi hai ki tumne mujhe ye naam dekar mere din ko kitna khaas bana diya hai."*

She laughed in her reply, her words playful. *"Shivu... it suits you. Ab toh tumhe isi naam se bulaya karungi."*

The thought of her calling him *"Shivu"* filled him with a warm excitement. It was as though she'd taken a piece of his heart, wrapping it gently with her own.

Their conversation drifted to lighter topics, teasing each other about their quirks and choices in music. Shivam shared a story about his sisters, recalling a time when they'd all tried to prank him, only for him to turn the prank on them. Vanshika laughed, her laughter ringing through his phone like a melody that was just for him.

"Tum toh bilkul shaitaan ho, Shivu," she typed, adding a playful emoji.

"Main sirf un logon ke saath shaitaan hoon jo mere dil ke kareeb hain," he replied, sending her a wink. He wanted her to know that she held a special place, even if he couldn't say it outright.

In a quiet moment, he typed a line that felt truer than anything else he'd said:

"Tum meri zindagi mein woh rang ho jo shayad mujhe kabhi akela mehsoos nahi hone dete."

Vanshika paused before replying, and Shivam's heart raced, wondering if he'd said too much. But when her response finally came, it was a simple, heartfelt message:

"Aur tum woh ho jo bina kahe mere dil ko samajh lete ho. Thank you, Shivam."

They ended the conversation with their usual "Radhe Radhe," but as Shivam lay in bed that night, he couldn't shake the feeling that this bond, this unspoken understanding, was something rare and beautiful.

Their bond had grown so naturally that Shivam sometimes forgot there was ever a time he didn't know Vanshika. Each conversation was like discovering a new part of her world, and he found himself wanting to be closer, to find a way to express just how much she meant to him.

One evening, as they chatted, Shivam found himself thinking about how he saw her—someone who had come into his life with an ease that felt like fate. On impulse, he decided to call her *"Vannu"* for the first time.

"You know, Vannu… tumhare bina life kaafi ajeeb si lagti hai," he typed, letting the new name settle between them.

There was a pause before she replied, and for a moment, he wondered if he'd gone too far. But then her response came, and he could almost hear the warmth in her voice.

"Vannu? Ab mujhe naye naam diye ja rahe hain?" she teased, adding a smiley face.

"Bas socha tumhare liye kuch khaas hona chahiye," he replied, hoping she understood that it was his way of making her a part of his life in a deeper way.

There was a quiet pause before she wrote back, her words soft but sincere. *"Mujhe yeh naya naam pasand aaya, Shivu. Thank you."*

For Shivam, her acceptance of the name felt like an unspoken affirmation. In that moment, he knew their bond had grown into something truly meaningful, something neither of them could easily explain.

As they continued talking, Shivam couldn't help but share a shayari that had been on his mind, one that captured how he felt:

"Tere naam ka ehsaas hai har uss lamhe mein, jo bas tere saath hi sukoon laata hai."

Her reply was instant, as if his words had touched something within her. *"Shayari bhi likhne lage ho, Shivu? Tum toh bilkul writer ho gaye."*

"Wahi ban raha hoon jo tumhare saath rehke banne ka mann karta hai," he replied, feeling a gentle joy at her response.

For the rest of the evening, they spoke as they always did, laughing and sharing stories, but something felt different. Shivam knew that this name, *"Vannu,"* held a new layer of affection, a symbol of the comfort and trust they had built. And as they ended their conversation with their usual *"Radhe Radhe,"* Shivam felt a quiet contentment settle in his heart.

He knew, without a doubt, that *"Vannu"* would be a name he'd cherish just as much as he cherished her.

With each day, Shivam and Vanshika's connection seemed to strengthen. Their conversations no longer required formality or restraint. They talked about everything and nothing, often veering into random memories or thoughts that brought them closer in unexpected ways. Their late-night chats had become an unspoken tradition, one Shivam cherished deeply.

One evening, while discussing their usual mix of songs and shared stories, Vanshika surprised him by sharing a personal moment.

"Aaj Himachali gaane suna rahi thi mummy," she texted, followed by a voice note of a familiar folk tune playing in the background. *"Sunke purani yaadein taaza ho gayi."*

Shivam felt a warmth spread through him as he listened, imagining her world through the sounds and memories she was sharing. *"It's beautiful, Vannu,"* he replied, appreciating the gentle melody and the piece of her life she was allowing him to see.

"Tumhe pasand aaya?" she asked, a hint of shyness in her message.

"Haan, pasand aaya... tumhara taste kaafi achha hai," he replied with sincerity, adding a smile. Shivam felt as though each conversation peeled back another layer, revealing a part of her he hadn't seen before.

Then, without thinking, he typed a line of shayari that had
been on his mind, something that felt perfect for the
moment:

*"Tere saath ke ye lamhe hai khaas, har pal mein tere hone
ka hai ehsaas."*

Vanshika's response was a simple *"Beautiful,"* but Shivam
could sense her smile through the screen. It was moments
like these that made him realize how much he valued her
presence, even in the smallest ways.

They continued talking, laughter punctuating their
exchanges as they teased each other about their quirks and
shared stories. Shivam shared a memory about his sisters
and how they always tried to prank him, only for him to
turn the tables. Vanshika's laughter echoed through the
chat, her happiness lighting up his evening.

"You're such a prankster, Shivu," she wrote, using his name
with a playful tone that made his heart race.

"Kya karoon, Vannu," he replied, grinning at the screen,
*"main bas apne un logo ke saath shaitani karta hoon jo
mere kareeb hain."*

As the night wore on, they fell into a comfortable silence,
each feeling the unspoken emotions that didn't need to be
put into words. They ended with their usual *"Radhe
Radhe,"* and as Shivam set his phone aside, he couldn't
help but feel that this bond, this friendship with *Vannu*, was
a rare treasure—one he would hold close for as long as he
could.

Their bond had a way of finding light even in the simplest moments, like the sunrise that Shivam would watch with a sense of peace after a late-night conversation with Vanshika. The messages they shared, the shayari, the inside jokes, had all become a part of his daily life, filling it with an unspoken joy that he hadn't known was missing.

One evening, as they chatted about random topics, Vanshika mentioned a childhood memory with her cousins, describing how they would spend summers together in Himachal, running around in the open fields, feeling free and limitless.

"Hamare woh masti bhare din... jaise zindagi uss waqt bilkul azaad thi," she typed, adding a thoughtful emoji.

Shivam replied, drawn to the image she painted. *"It sounds like paradise, Vannu. Sometimes I feel like I missed out by never experiencing that side of life."*

"Agar tum tab hote toh tumhe woh sab dikhati," she replied warmly, *"but maybe there's still time to share that part of me with you."*

The words stayed with Shivam. He could feel the sincerity in her message, the unspoken invitation she extended. There was something about her that felt like home—a place he hadn't visited but felt he belonged to.

Inspired, he wrote her a short shayari:

"Tere saath woh mehsoos hota hai jo kabhi kahin nahi hua, Jaise tere saaye mein apni hi kahani likh raha hoon main."

Vanshika responded with a simple heart, and they continued talking, her words lingering with him long after the conversation had ended. As they shared stories, he found himself admiring her courage, her spirit, and the way she held onto her roots. There was a strength in her that fascinated him, a quiet resilience that reminded him of the very mountains she had grown up admiring.

Suddenly, Vanshika's message broke into his thoughts:

"Shivam, kabhi kabhi lagta hai zindagi humare plans se alag chalti hai," she wrote, her words carrying a touch of introspection.

"Hmm," he replied, thinking carefully. *"But maybe those unexpected paths lead us to the most beautiful places."*

There was a pause before her reply, as if she were taking in his words. *"Shayad tum sahi keh rahe ho. Life really has a way of surprising us, Shivu."*

For Shivam, her use of "Shivu" felt like an affirmation of their growing closeness, a reminder that they had built something precious between them. He didn't need to tell her how much she meant to him; her presence was enough, and in moments like these, he realized that it was all he truly needed.

They ended their conversation, as always, with *"Radhe Radhe,"* a ritual that felt comforting, like a promise to be there for each other, no matter where life took them.

As he set his phone down, Shivam lay back, a quiet smile on his face. In his heart, he knew that he had found something rare in *Vannu*, something that didn't need to be named to be understood.

The connection between Shivam and Vanshika had settled into a place that felt natural, almost as if they'd known each other forever. Each conversation seemed to bring them closer, and Shivam found himself savoring every moment, every word she shared. Her presence had become a quiet comfort, a part of his day he looked forward to more than anything else.

One evening, as they were chatting, Shivam sent her a message that carried a playful tone but held a deeper meaning beneath it.

"Vannu, tumhara aur mera routine toh ab bilkul fix ho gaya hai," he typed, followed by a winking emoji. *"Itna yaad mat karo, warna aadat ban jayegi."*

Her response came instantly, playful but with a hint of sincerity. *"Woh toh pehle hi ban gayi hai, Shivu. Tumhaare bina thoda ajeeb lagta hai."*

A surge of warmth flooded through Shivam at her words. There was something so endearing, so comforting, about the way she openly shared her feelings, even if they were tucked behind her playful words. In that moment, he realized how much he valued these quiet exchanges, the subtle ways they both hinted at emotions they weren't yet ready to name.

He thought about how natural it felt to be with her, how even their silences had a warmth that made him feel at home. Deciding to capture his thoughts, he sent her a short line that felt truer than anything else he could say:

"Tere hone ka ehsaas hi kaafi hai, aur kuch kehne ki zaroorat nahi."

She read it, and after a brief pause, responded with a heart emoji, and Shivam could almost picture her soft smile on the other side of the screen. For him, every moment with *Vannu* felt like a step into something deeper, a space where neither of them needed to speak their emotions aloud to understand them.

They continued talking, discussing memories and dreams of the future. Vanshika shared her ambitions, the things she wanted to accomplish, and Shivam listened intently, feeling privileged to be trusted with her hopes. She painted a picture of a life she wanted, a world she envisioned, and Shivam could see himself in it, though he kept that part to himself.

As they wrapped up the evening conversation, Vanshika sent him one last message:

"Goodnight, Shivu. Tumhe yaad kar ke sona bhi ek alag sukoon deta hai. Radhe Radhe."

His heart skipped a beat at her words. For Shivam, that simple message meant more than he could express, and he knew that *Vannu* had become an inseparable part of his world. He typed back, *"Goodnight, Vannu. Radhe Radhe."*

And as he closed his eyes, he felt a contentment he hadn't known he needed.

Shivam's life seemed to brighten with every conversation he shared with Vanshika. The routine of chatting late into the night, exchanging stories, jokes, and fleeting thoughts, had become a part of him. Her words lingered with him long after their conversations ended, filling his days with a quiet joy that felt like his own little secret.

One evening, they found themselves reminiscing about the time they first met, recalling every little detail. Vanshika described her perspective with a teasing smile in her words.

"Tumhe yaad hai, pehli baar jab hum mile the, tum kitne nervous the?" she texted, adding a laughing emoji.

Shivam grinned as he remembered that day, feeling a mix of nostalgia and warmth. *"Haan, of course yaad hai! Tumse milna kuch alag hi tha, Vannu. Woh shyness bhi ek tarah ka excitement hi tha,"* he admitted, feeling comfortable enough to confess this now.

"Mujhe toh pehle se hi lagta tha ki tum thode se shy ho," she replied, *"lekin uss din tum waise nahi lage. Tumhare expression bilkul clear the."*

He laughed, typing back, *"Woh toh tumhara hi effect tha."* In truth, Shivam had always found Vanshika to be someone he couldn't fully predict, and perhaps that was part of her charm—the way she brought out new sides of him without even trying.

Feeling a burst of inspiration, he decided to send her a line of shayari that had been lingering in his mind:

*"Pehli mulaqat ka woh pal yaad hai mujhe,
Jaise uss lamhe ne mere dil mein rang bhar diye hain tere
saaye se."*

She paused before responding, her reply as heartfelt as ever.
*"Shivu, tumhari baatein hamesha kuch khaas si lagti hain.
Tum waise ho jaisa maine kabhi socha nahi tha."*

Their conversation drifted from that first meeting to their
dreams, hopes, and what they wanted in life. Vanshika
shared her goals, her love for simple joys, and Shivam
listened with his full attention, feeling a deep admiration
for the way she carried herself.

It was in moments like these that he realized how deeply he
respected her—not just for the way she was with him, but
for the strength, resilience, and warmth she brought to
everyone around her.

They said goodnight as they always did, with a gentle
"Radhe Radhe," and Shivam found himself lying in bed,
replaying their conversation in his mind. This feeling, this
connection—he couldn't imagine his life without it.

In his heart, he knew that what they shared was more than
friendship, and perhaps, one day, they would both find the
words to say it out loud. For now, it was enough to have
Vannu in his life, to hold onto these moments like a
precious secret, a quiet joy that belonged to both of them.

Shivam found himself savoring every word they shared, every late-night message that lingered in his heart long after it was sent. Vanshika had become more than just a friend—she was a presence he looked forward to, a part of his life that brought meaning to even the simplest moments.

One night, as they chatted, Vanshika opened up about her dreams, speaking of her love for Himachal and her desire to carry forward her family's traditions while also creating her own path. Shivam listened intently, drawn to the passion in her words.

"Sometimes, Vannu, I feel like I've known you my entire life," he admitted softly, almost to himself. *"Yeh rishta bas dosti se kuch zyada lagta hai, jaise humara connection kuch alag hi ho."*

She took a moment before replying, her words carrying a sincerity that Shivam could feel deeply. *"Kabhi kabhi mujhe bhi aisa lagta hai, Shivu. Tumhare saath sab kuch simple aur real lagta hai, bina kisi pretension ke."*

A warmth spread through him at her response. There was something in the honesty of her words that felt like a silent promise, an unspoken understanding that existed between them.

Feeling a surge of emotion, he typed out another shayari, a line that had been on his mind:

*"Tere saath ke kuch pal yunhi bas guzar jayein,
Jaise zindagi ko ab aur kuch kehne ki zaroorat na ho."*

She replied with a quiet, *"That's beautiful, Shivu,"* and for a moment, they both let the silence speak for them. It was as if they'd reached a place where words weren't necessary, where their bond was strong enough to hold them together without explanation.

After a while, they said their goodnights, ending with their familiar *"Radhe Radhe,"* a ritual that felt like their own little tradition.

As Shivam lay in bed that night, he knew that whatever this was between them, it was something he wanted to hold onto, something that had become as precious as life itself. He didn't need to say it out loud—his heart knew that *Vannu* was someone special, someone who had become a part of him in ways he hadn't anticipated.

And with that thought, he drifted into a peaceful sleep, content in the knowledge that, for now, this bond was more than enough.

The Beginning of Us

After Shivam's confession, things had remained steady but unspoken between them. Shivam respected Vanshika's boundaries, knowing she needed time to process her own feelings, and he'd told himself that her friendship was enough. Yet, over time, Shivam sensed a quiet change in her—the way she would hold onto their conversations a little longer, the softness in her voice when she spoke to him.

One evening, as they chatted, Vanshika's words took on a different tone, a tenderness that Shivam hadn't felt from her before.

"Shivu," she began slowly, *"pichli baar tumne jo kaha tha… woh ab tak mere dil mein hai."*

Shivam's heart raced, remembering the confession he'd shared with her before, the one she had gently declined. He'd accepted it, hoping that someday she might feel the same way. Now, hearing her bring it up felt like a small opening, one he hadn't dared to expect.

"Pata hai, uss waqt main ready nahi thi… aur sach mein lagta tha ke relationships se door rehna hi sahi hai," she admitted, her words carrying a hint of vulnerability. *"Par tumhare saath jo connection mehsoos kiya, usne mujhe yeh sochne par majboor kar diya ke shayad main galat thi."*

Shivam felt an overwhelming sense of hope bloom within him. *"Vannu, tumhe pata hai tum mere liye kya ho, lekin main chahta hoon ke tum yeh khud feel karo, bina kisi pressure ke."*

She paused before replying, as if gathering her thoughts. *"Shivam, tum wo insaan ho jo mere saath ho toh sab kuch poora lagta hai… aur ab main ready hoon yeh maanna ko ki shayad yeh rishta mujhe bhi chahiye."*

Her confession was simple yet powerful, a quiet acknowledgment of the love that had grown between them over time. Shivam could barely contain his joy, feeling a rush of gratitude for the moment he'd been waiting for.

"Toh ab hum dono officially kuch hain?" he asked, his words laced with both excitement and disbelief.

"Haan, Shivu," she replied, a shy smile in her words. *"Ab hum dono ek saath hain… aur yehi mere liye kaafi hai."*

The weight of her words settled around them, filling the silence with an indescribable warmth. They both felt the joy of finally being together, the sense of rightness in each other's presence. For Shivam, this was a moment he knew he would remember forever—a turning point in their journey, from friendship to something much deeper.

As they shared laughter and promises for this new beginning, Shivam felt his world align in ways he'd only dreamed of. He knew that with *Vannu* by his side, he was ready to face anything.

With their feelings finally confessed, Shivam and Vanshika found themselves basking in a new kind of happiness. Every message, every glance felt different now—there was an unspoken thrill in simply knowing they were together. The conversations that had once been careful and tentative were now filled with playful affection, a sense of belonging that warmed them both.

The evening after their confession, Shivam couldn't contain his excitement. As they talked, he let his happiness show in every message, knowing that for once, he didn't have to hold back.

"Vannu," he wrote, his words laced with a gentle tease, *"ab toh tum officially meri ho, toh main tumhe thoda tang kar sakta hoon, right?"*

She replied with a laughing emoji, her words playful. *"Tum pehle bhi kam nahi karte the, Shivu!"* Then, after a pause, she added, *"Lekin ab shayad yeh tang karna mujhe aur bhi pasand hai."*

Shivam grinned at her message, feeling the warmth of her words sink in. It was as if the weight they'd been carrying, the hesitation and unspoken feelings, had finally lifted, leaving behind a lightness that filled him with joy.

As they continued talking, their conversation naturally drifted to how things had changed between them.

"Pehle toh kabhi nahi socha tha ke hum dono yahan tak pahunch jaayenge," Vanshika admitted softly. *"Woh shayad*

*isiliye kyunki uss waqt main taiyaar nahi thi... lekin ab
tumhare bina zindagi sochna mushkil lagta hai."*

Shivam felt his heart swell at her words, his admiration for
her growing even more. He took a deep breath and replied
with the honesty he knew she deserved.

*"Vannu, tum mere liye woh ho jo kabhi kisi aur mein nahi
mili. Tumhare saath, har chhoti baat bhi itni khaas lagti
hai. Ab toh tum meri ho, aur main tumhara."*

Her response was simple, yet it carried all the emotion he
could have hoped for: *"Haan, Shivu. Ab toh hum dono ek
saath hain."*

They spent the rest of the evening talking about everything
and nothing, laughing at inside jokes, planning imaginary
trips, and teasing each other in a way that felt like second
nature. Shivam couldn't remember a time he'd felt so at
ease, so completely understood. For once, he didn't have to
explain himself—*Vannu* just got him, in a way that made
him feel both grateful and amazed.

As they finally said their goodnights, Vanshika sent him a
message that stayed with him long after the conversation
had ended:

*"Shivu, tum mere liye woh ho jo zindagi ko aur bhi
khubsurat bana deta hai. Thank you for being you."*

Shivam read her message one last time before setting his
phone aside, his heart full. For the first time, he felt
complete, as if everything had fallen into place. He drifted
into sleep, knowing that whatever challenges lay ahead,

they would face them together, and that thought brought him a peace he hadn't known before.

The following days felt like a dream for Shivam. Knowing that Vanshika was his—and he was hers—filled his world with a newfound brightness. Each conversation, each message, carried a special warmth now, like every moment with her was a memory being etched into his heart.

One afternoon, as they exchanged messages, Vanshika playfully texted him, *"So, Shivu, ab tum officially mera tang karne ka haq rakhte ho, lekin yaad rahe, I'm no easy target."* She added a winking emoji, her tone light yet affectionate.

Shivam laughed, his fingers tapping a quick response. *"Challenge accepted, Vannu. Tumhe pata nahi hai ki ab tumhara Shivu tumhe kitna tang karne waala hai!"*

She replied with a laughing emoji, and Shivam could imagine her laughter, bright and free, filling her room. Their dynamic had always been filled with teasing and playfulness, but now, with their mutual feelings in the open, it had deepened into something much more meaningful.

Feeling the moment, he decided to share something personal, a thought that had been on his mind since their confession. *"Vannu, tumhare bina pehle zindagi ek thoda ajeeb sa silence thi. Tum aayi aur sab kuch ek melody ban gaya."*

Vanshika's reply came after a few moments. *"Aur tum wo ho, Shivu, jo bina kuch kehkar bhi mujhe samajh lete ho. Shayad isi wajah se mujhe tumhara saath itna special lagta hai."*

As they continued to talk, Shivam felt a surge of gratitude. He had always known that *Vannu* was special, but being with her, being able to share these honest feelings, made him feel as if he'd finally found his place in the world.

Then, in a gentle shift, their conversation turned to the idea of keeping their relationship private, at least for now. They both agreed that they didn't need to share this part of their lives with everyone just yet. Shivam, however, felt the need to clarify.

"Par Vannu, Harsh ko kabhi toh pata chalega," he wrote, remembering how close he and Harsh had always been. *"Woh hum dono ke baare mein toh zaroor poochta rahega."*

"Haan, main samajh rahi hoon," Vanshika replied, *"lekin filhaal mujhe yeh apna chhota sa secret rakha zyada achha lagta hai... sirf tum aur main."*

Shivam understood her sentiment perfectly. The idea of keeping this love private, like a hidden treasure only they knew about, brought an unexpected thrill. He replied with a smile, *"Theek hai, sirf tum aur main. Ab yeh hamara chhota sa raaz hai."*

For the rest of the afternoon, they spoke in soft tones, sharing dreams and secrets they'd never told anyone else. Shivam could feel the depth of her trust, and in that trust, he found a joy he hadn't known before.

As they ended their conversation with their familiar *"Radhe Radhe,"* Shivam felt his heart swell with happiness. Their love, quiet and true, was something he cherished deeply, and he knew that whatever lay ahead, this connection would always be their own, cherished and protected.

The days that followed felt like something out of a dream for Shivam. Every time he spoke to Vanshika, he found himself falling deeper, savoring each message and every little exchange as though it were a treasure.

One night, after a long, lighthearted conversation, Vanshika's message came through just as he was about to say goodnight.

"Radhe Radhe, Shivu," she wrote, adding a sleepy emoji. *"Tumhare bina ab toh sona bhi ajeeb lagta hai."*

He felt his heart race, a smile spreading across his face as he replied, *"Radhe Radhe, meri Vannu. Tumhare bina subah ka message na aaye toh din thoda adhoora sa lagta hai."*

She responded with a soft, *"Good night, mendak,"* throwing in the nickname she'd recently given him. Shivam grinned, loving the affectionate humor she'd brought into their relationship.

"Good night, meri chudail," he replied with a wink, feeling a thrill in using the name he'd playfully given her. He knew she'd laugh at the playful banter, and her reply did not disappoint.

"Love you, Shivu," she wrote, her words carrying a simple but powerful warmth that filled him with joy.

"Love you too, Vannu," he replied, the words easy and true, and as they exchanged hearts and laughing emojis, Shivam felt a happiness he hadn't known before.

Their routine had developed a rhythm now, one that included morning texts and late-night goodnights with "Radhe Radhe" and "Love you" sent back and forth. It was a small ritual that had quickly become a part of his day, something he looked forward to with anticipation.

Sometimes, Vanshika would tease him with stories about her day or pretend to be busy, only to reveal she'd been thinking of him all along. She knew exactly how to keep Shivam guessing, a lighthearted game that always ended with her reassurance.

"Tumhaara mendak bhi thoda jalta hai, you know," he wrote with a playful tone after one of her teasing messages.

She replied instantly with a laughing emoji, *"Achha sorry baba! Tumhe tang karne mein mazaa aata hai."*

"Tum hi ho, meri chudail," he typed, feeling the words settle warmly in his heart.

As they ended the night with their usual *"Radhe Radhe, Good night, Love you,"* Shivam lay in bed, his heart full of the little exchanges, the jokes, the promises that filled their days. For him, these small moments were everything; they were proof that he'd found something rare, something he would hold onto forever.

Their relationship settled into a beautiful rhythm, with late-night chats and early-morning messages filling Shivam's days with a quiet joy. Each "Radhe Radhe," each "Good night, love you," felt like a small promise they shared, a comfort that made Shivam's heart feel full.

One evening, as they exchanged messages, Vanshika surprised him with a question that felt both playful and sincere.

"Shivu, kabhi tumne socha hai, hum dono ki kahani kaisi lagti hai?" she asked, her words carrying a hint of curiosity.

Shivam thought for a moment before responding, letting a small smile play on his lips as he typed. *"Humari kahani bilkul tumhari tarah hai, Vannu—simple, sweet, aur thodi unpredictable."*

Her reply was instant, filled with laughter. *"Unpredictable? Yeh tumne sahi kaha. Tumhare saath sab kuch thoda unexpected lagta hai."*

They both laughed, and the conversation flowed into memories they'd shared—times when Vanshika had teased him, or moments when he'd found himself smiling for no reason just because she was there. It was as if they were reliving their story together, piecing each memory into a tapestry that told of the journey from friendship to love.

"Waise," Shivam typed, *"tum meri zindagi mein bilkul waise aayi jaise ek adhoore gaane mein sur aata hai."*

Vanshika responded with a heart emoji, then sent a voice message: *"Shivu, tum jo bhi kehte ho, woh mere dil ko bahut sukoon deta hai. Tum ho toh sab kuch bas perfect lagta hai."*

Hearing her voice, so soft and sincere, Shivam felt a warmth fill his chest. He knew that these moments were special, that every word they shared held a weight that only they could understand.

"Vannu, tum mere liye sirf ek dost ya partner nahi ho," he replied thoughtfully. *"Tum woh ho jo mujhe poora mehsoos karati ho, jaise mere dil ki har kami tum se hi puri hoti hai."*

The message lingered between them, each of them feeling the depth of the words unspoken. After a few moments, Vanshika responded simply, *"Aur tum mere liye woh ho jo bina kuch kahe mujhe samajh sakta hai."*

They ended their night with their usual *"Radhe Radhe, Good night, love you,"* a small ritual that had quickly become the highlight of Shivam's day. As he lay in bed, he felt a quiet contentment settle over him, knowing that he had found something precious in *Vannu*—something that needed no explanations, only the gentle assurance of their bond.

As days turned into weeks, Shivam and Vanshika's connection only grew deeper. Each conversation, each shared laugh, felt like a small piece of the world they were building together. Shivam found himself constantly thinking of her, looking forward to every notification from *Vannu,* knowing she'd bring a smile to his face no matter what.

One night, as they chatted late into the evening, Vanshika sent a message that made Shivam's heart skip a beat.

"Kabhi kabhi sochti hoon, Shivu, tumhare bina life kitni alag hoti. Tum ho toh sab kuch kitna simple aur acha lagta hai."

Shivam felt his heart race. Her words held a weight he hadn't expected, a tenderness that made him feel as though he was truly understood. He took a deep breath, replying with all the honesty he felt.

"Meri zindagi bhi tumhare bina bilkul adhoori lagti hai, Vannu. Tum wo ho jo mere har din ko khubsurat banati ho."

She responded with a soft, *"Tumhe yeh bolte hue sunna mujhe acha lagta hai, mendak,"* adding a laughing emoji. Shivam's grin widened at her use of the nickname—*mendak*—a term she'd used often, one that made their bond feel even more intimate and uniquely theirs.

Their conversation drifted naturally into the little moments they'd shared, the memories that now held so much more meaning. Vanshika shared her dreams and plans, and

Shivam found himself listening intently, feeling honored that she trusted him with her hopes.

"Kabhi kabhi lagta hai, yeh sab ek sapna hai," Shivam admitted, his words soft but sincere. *"Tumhare saath har baat, har moment bas itna perfect lagta hai ki sach mein yakin nahi hota."*

Vanshika's reply was quick, her words carrying the same warmth he felt. *"Shivu, tum mere liye woh ho jo sirf mere sapnon mein tha. Tumhaare saath sab kuch sahi lagta hai."*

They ended their conversation, as they always did, with *"Radhe Radhe, Good night, lovee you,"* the words a gentle reassurance of their connection. As Shivam lay in bed, he felt an overwhelming sense of gratitude, knowing that he had found someone who understood him so completely, who shared in his dreams and his laughter.

For the first time, he felt a certainty he hadn't known before—a quiet realization that he had found something he would hold onto forever, a love that felt as timeless as it was true.

The days seemed to pass in a blur of shared moments and gentle affection. Shivam and Vanshika had found a rhythm that felt easy and fulfilling, a comfort that came from knowing they were there for each other. Each morning text and late-night goodbye was a reminder of the joy they'd found together.

One evening, as they chatted, Shivam noticed that Vanshika's replies were a bit delayed. Concerned, he typed a quick message.

"Sab theek hai na, Vannu? Aaj tum thodi slow lag rahi ho."

There was a pause before her response came through, *"Haan, Shivu, bas aaj kuch thakawat si mehsoos ho rahi hai."*

Shivam immediately felt a wave of worry wash over him. He knew she often neglected to take her medication on time, and his instinct to care for her took over.

"Vannu, tumne apni medicine time par li hai na?" he asked, his tone gentle but firm.

She replied with a sheepish emoji, *"Umm... bas bhool gayi thi aaj, lekin abhi le rahi hoon. Tum bhi na, ek reminder ho bilkul."*

Shivam felt a mix of relief and amusement. *"Haan, reminder hi samajh lo mujhe. Tum apna khayal nahi rakhti toh mujhe tension hota hai."*

Her next message made his heart warm. *"Tumhara ye care mujhe bahut special feel karwata hai, mendak."* It was her way of acknowledging his affection, and Shivam couldn't help but smile at her words.

As they continued chatting, Vanshika began to open up about her day, sharing little moments that had made her laugh and times when she'd thought of him. Shivam listened, feeling a deeper connection with each word. He realized that, beyond the titles and names, they were building something real, something rooted in mutual respect and care.

Just before saying goodnight, Vanshika typed one last message that Shivam would hold onto long after their conversation ended.

"Shivu, tum mere liye sirf ek dost nahi, tum wo ho jo mujhe pura mehsoos karata hai. Tumhare bina life kaafi incomplete lagti hai."

Shivam's reply came easily, without hesitation. *"Vannu, tum meri zindagi ka wo hissa ho jo main khud bhi nahi samajh sakta, lekin tumhare saath sab kuch sahi lagta hai."*

They ended their chat with the familiar ritual: *"Radhe Radhe, Good night, love you."* Shivam lay back, feeling the weight of their words settle around him. For the first time, he felt the power of what they'd built—a love that went beyond words, grounded in shared moments, unspoken care, and a future they were ready to face together.

Their relationship had quickly become the anchor in Shivam's life, bringing a sense of comfort and joy that felt as natural as breathing. Every day seemed filled with warmth, laughter, and moments that made him feel closer to *Vannu* in ways he hadn't anticipated.

One afternoon, while they were chatting, Vanshika brought up her close friend, Sanjana.

"Shivu, mujhe tumhe apni ek aur friend se milwana hai—Sanjana," she typed, her excitement clear in her message. *"Wo meri school friend hai, aur usne mere baare mein bahut kuch suna hai tumse related."*

Shivam felt a smile spread across his face, intrigued by the idea of meeting one of Vanshika's close friends. *"Achha? Toh Sanjana ko bhi humari story ke bare mein pata hai?"*

"Haan, woh meri woh wali friend hai jisse main sab kuch share karti hoon," Vanshika replied with a wink emoji. *"Aur wo tumhe milne ke liye bahut excited hai."*

A few days later, the three of them joined an online chat, and Shivam was immediately drawn to Sanjana's cheerful and friendly nature. She teased Vanshika playfully, and her warmth made him feel as if he'd known her for years.

"Toh ye hain humare Shivu," Sanjana began with a grin, *"jo tumhare bina humari Vanshu ko sukoon se sone bhi nahi dete."*

Shivam laughed, feeling a little embarrassed yet happy to be accepted by someone so close to Vanshika. *"Haan, bas*

Vanshu ko tang karna mera haq hai ab," he replied, sending a winking emoji toward Vanshika.

Their conversations soon became a fun addition to Shivam and Vanshika's relationship. Sanjana's playful teasing and the way she talked about her memories with Vanshika brought Shivam even closer to understanding the girl he was falling for. Through these conversations, he also felt a sense of support—a bond that connected him not just to Vanshika but to the people who loved her as well.

As the evening wore on and their goodbyes came around, Vanshika sent him a message.

"Radhe Radhe, Shivu. Thank you for being so good with my friends—it means a lot."

He replied gently, *"Radhe Radhe, Vannu. Tumhari life ka hissa banne mein mujhe bahut khushi milti hai."*

The conversation ended, as always, with their familiar *"Good night, love you."* But as Shivam lay in bed, he felt the bond between them deepen, knowing that he was gradually becoming a part of her world in a way he hadn't expected. And with each shared moment, each new connection, he realized just how much he wanted this feeling to last.

In the days that followed, Shivam's connection with Vanshika deepened. With Sanjana now included in some of their conversations, Shivam felt a greater sense of belonging, as if he were gradually becoming part of Vanshika's inner world. He enjoyed the small group chats, the teasing and laughter that filled his evenings, and the shared memories that made him feel closer to *Vannu* with every conversation.

One evening, as the three of them chatted, Sanjana brought up a moment from their school days.

"Waise, Shivam, tumhe pata hai, Vanshu school mein kitni shy hua karti thi?" Sanjana teased, adding a laughing emoji. *"Lekin tumhare saath toh bilkul alag hi lagti hai."*

Shivam chuckled, looking over at Vanshika's message. *"Achha, toh mere saath aane ke baad hi asli Vanshu bahar aayi?"*

"Haan, tumhara asar kaafi hua hai, Shivu," Vanshika replied with a wink, her tone playful yet carrying a sincerity he'd come to love.

These small exchanges brought Shivam immense happiness. He could feel how much they had both changed since meeting each other, and it made their relationship feel even more special. For Shivam, *Vannu* was no longer just a friend or a companion—she was the person who made his world feel whole.

Later that night, after Sanjana had logged off, Vanshika and Shivam continued their private chat, their conversation taking on a softer tone.

"Shivu," Vanshika typed, her message carrying a gentleness he adored, *"pata hai, tumne meri life mein jo khushi aur sukoon laaya hai, woh pehle kabhi nahi tha."*

Shivam felt his heart swell at her words. *"Vannu, tumne bhi mujhe wo feeling di hai jo main kabhi kisi ke saath feel nahi kar sakta."*

They stayed in that quiet, contented moment, each feeling the depth of the bond they had created. The night ended as it always did—with *"Radhe Radhe, Good night, love you"* exchanged between them.

As Shivam closed his eyes, he felt an overwhelming sense of gratitude for the love they shared. With *Vannu* by his side, he knew that every day was a chance to create memories, to cherish the simple moments, and to hold onto the happiness they had found in each other.

As Shivam and Vanshika continued to grow closer, their bond became a source of joy and strength in their lives. With every shared story, late-night message, and whispered "lovee you," they had created a world that felt unbreakable.

One evening, as they exchanged messages, Vanshika brought up something that made Shivam smile.

"Shivu," she began, *"tumne kabhi socha hai humara future kaisa hoga?"*

Shivam took a moment to think, the thought of a future with Vanshika filling him with warmth. He typed back, *"Haan, Vannu. Tumhare saath ek life imagine karna bahut natural lagta hai."*

Vanshika's reply was instant. *"Mujhe bhi lagta hai ke tumhare bina kuch adhura sa hai… aur shayad hum dono ka yeh bond hamesha aise hi rahe."*

Shivam's heart raced as he read her words. He realized how deeply she felt for him, and it only strengthened his love for her. For a moment, they both lingered in that silence, letting their mutual dreams of the future drift between them.

Before saying goodnight, Vanshika wrote one final message: *"Shivam, tum meri zindagi ka wo hissa ho jo main kabhi khona nahi chahti."*

He replied with a simple yet heartfelt message, *"Aur tum meri ho, Vannu. Hamesha ke liye."*

They ended the conversation with their ritual, each whispering *"Radhe Radhe, Good night, love you,"* a promise sealed by the words they'd come to cherish.

Navigating the Unexpected and Growing Tension

Shivam and Vanshika had created a bond so close, so deep, that it felt as though nothing could ever come between them. Their days were filled with laughter, support, and shared dreams for the future, each conversation adding layers to the connection they had built.

One evening, as they were chatting about their plans for the coming months, Vanshika texted, *"Shivu, sometimes I wonder... if we were actually together every day, wouldn't life feel perfect?"*

Shivam smiled, feeling a familiar warmth at her words. *"Haan, Vannu, bilkul. I'd give anything for that. But even now, it already feels like you're with me all the time."*

She replied with a heart emoji, her response thoughtful. *"True, but imagine getting to see you in person. I think I'd be all shy again, like when we first met."*

"Acha? Toh phir mujhe tumhe comfortable feel karwana padega, just like the first time," he teased, picturing her shy smile as he typed.

Their conversation turned to memories, both of them laughing and sharing little moments that had come to define their relationship. Just as they began to say goodnight, Vanshika brought up something new.

"By the way, Shivu," she started, *"I was thinking… maybe you could meet my cousin, Deepanshi, and my friend, Sanjana? I think you'd really get along with them."*

Shivam felt a thrill of excitement. He knew how close Vanshika was to both Deepanshi and Sanjana, and being introduced felt like a meaningful step. *"I'd love to meet them, Vannu. I want to know everyone who's important to you."*

Her reply was instant, with a laughing emoji: *"Just wait till you meet them! They'll probably have a hundred questions about us."*

"I'm ready!" he replied with a wink. *"Bring on the questions, I'm all yours."*

They ended the night with their familiar ritual: *"Radhe Radhe, Good night, love you,"* words that had become their way of holding onto each other, even in the quiet hours.

As Shivam lay back in bed, he felt a deep satisfaction in knowing that he was becoming more integrated into Vanshika's life, connecting with the people she cherished. And with every shared laugh, every invitation into her world, he felt their relationship grow stronger.

With Sanjana and Deepanshi now part of his life, Shivam found himself enjoying their group chats. Vanshika, Shivam, and her two close friends would often message in the evenings, sharing jokes, teasing each other, and exchanging stories that made Shivam feel completely at ease and a little closer to Vanshika's world.

One evening, as they were chatting about their plans for the weekend, Sanjana messaged, *"So, Shivam, I hear you're always reminding Vanshu about her meds and everything else. You're basically her personal reminder, huh?"*

Shivam laughed, typing back, *"Well, someone has to make sure she's taking care of herself! Just doing my part."*

Deepanshi joined in, *"Good work, Shivam! Vanshu definitely needs it sometimes. You're like her official life manager now."*

Vanshika responded with a laughing emoji, clearly enjoying the playful teasing. *"Arrey bas karo tum log. Tum dono aur Shivam milke mujhe bahut zyada pampered feel karwa rahe ho!"*

Shivam smiled at the messages, feeling grateful for the warmth and acceptance in the group. Their conversations added depth to his relationship with Vanshika, making him feel as if he was truly becoming a part of her life.

Later that night, after the group chat had quieted down, Vanshika messaged him privately.

"Shivu, I hope my friends aren't teasing you too much," she wrote with a winking emoji.

"Not at all, Vannu," he replied warmly. *"I'm just glad to know the people who mean so much to you."*

They ended the night with their usual *"Radhe Radhe, Good night, love you,"* a nightly ritual Shivam had come to cherish deeply. As he lay in bed, he felt a sense of belonging, knowing that Vanshika's friends had welcomed him with open hearts.

As time went on, Shivam found himself growing closer not only to Vanshika but also to the people she cared about. The group chats with Sanjana and Deepanshi had become a regular part of his life, and he appreciated the lightheartedness they brought to his days. It felt as though he'd been welcomed into a little community built around shared laughter, inside jokes, and quiet support.

One evening, after Vanshika had gone offline for a bit, Sanjana messaged him privately.

"Hey, Shivam," she began, her tone friendlier than usual. *"I just wanted to say, Vanshu's really happy with you. She doesn't say it outright, but it's obvious."*

Shivam felt a warmth settle over him, grateful for Sanjana's words. *"Thanks, Sanjana. She means the world to me, so I'm glad she's happy too."*

"I know," she replied with a heart emoji. *"Just make sure to keep making her smile. She deserves it."*

That small interaction left Shivam feeling more deeply connected to Vanshika's world than ever before. Knowing that her friends were rooting for them added a quiet strength to the bond he and Vanshika shared.

Later that night, Vanshika messaged him, her words carrying the playful tone he'd come to adore.

"Shivu, tum mujhse itni baatein karte ho, tumhe kabhi bore nahi hota?" she teased.

"Bore? Kabhi nahi, Vannu," he replied, smiling as he typed. *"Tumhare saath toh har baat special lagti hai."*

She responded with a heart, and he could feel her warmth across the miles that separated them.

They ended their conversation, as they always did, with *"Radhe Radhe, Good night, love you,"* words that had become like a lullaby for Shivam, grounding him at the end of each day. As he drifted off to sleep, he felt a sense of contentment that was hard to put into words. With Vanshika by his side, everything felt brighter, simpler, and endlessly fulfilling.

Days passed, and Shivam continued to cherish every moment he shared with Vanshika. They had created a little world of their own—one filled with lighthearted conversations, affectionate teasing, and silent promises that needed no words. Shivam found himself looking forward to every message from her, knowing that she'd bring a smile to his face, no matter what.

One evening, as they were chatting about their day, Vanshika brought up an incident that had left her a bit frustrated.

"Aaj classes ke baad kuch ajeeb hua," she began, adding an annoyed emoji. *"There was this guy who kept asking if I was single. I told him I wasn't interested, but he just didn't get it."*

Shivam felt a slight pang of jealousy, but he quickly pushed it aside, focusing instead on her words. *"Oh? And did you set him straight, meri chudail?"*

She laughed at the nickname, replying, *"Of course, Shivu! Tumhare alawa kisi aur ke liye interest kaha hai?"* She added a heart, her message filled with sincerity.

"Good to know!" he replied with a wink. *"But next time, let me know if anyone bothers you. Tumhara mendak bhi kuch kaam aayega."*

Their playful banter continued, and Shivam felt a warmth spread through him, knowing that they both shared this sense of protectiveness and loyalty toward each other. It was a reminder of how much they meant to each other, even in the little things.

Just as they were about to end the conversation, Vanshika sent him a message that made his heart skip a beat.

"You know, Shivu," she wrote, *"sometimes it feels like I've known you forever. It's like you're a part of me."*

Shivam took a deep breath, feeling the weight of her words settle around him. *"Same here, Vannu. Tum meri zindagi ka woh hissa ho jo main kabhi kho nahi sakta. It's like I was waiting for you this whole time."*

They ended the night, as always, with *"Radhe Radhe, Good night, love you,"* a ritual that had become the most comforting part of Shivam's day. As he lay in bed, he replayed her words in his mind, feeling a depth of emotion that went beyond anything he'd ever experienced. For him, Vanshika was no longer just a part of his life—she was the center of it, the anchor that kept him grounded and hopeful.

As days turned into weeks, Shivam and Vanshika settled into a rhythm of shared affection and daily moments that felt like small promises. Each conversation was a reminder of how close they had become, and for Shivam, every message, every "Radhe Radhe, Good night, love you" was like a thread weaving their lives together.

One afternoon, Vanshika sent him a message that carried a hint of nostalgia.

"Shivu, do you remember how shy we were when we first started talking? Can't believe how much things have changed."

Shivam smiled as he read her words, memories flashing in his mind. *"Haan, I remember that day perfectly. Tumhara woh thoda sa hesitant smile ab bhi yaad hai."*

Vanshika laughed, replying, *"Arrey, woh toh tumhari wajah se tha! Tumne pehle hi din mujhe aise tang karna shuru kar diya tha."*

"Are wah! Tum bhi toh ab tang karne mein master ban gayi ho, Vannu," he replied with a laughing emoji.

They continued reminiscing about the early days, laughing over their initial awkwardness and the small misunderstandings that had now become cherished memories. It was as though they'd been given a chance to relive those early moments, seeing how far they had come together.

Just as their chat began winding down, Vanshika sent him a message that caught him off guard.

"Shivu, tum mere liye itne important ho gaye ho... kabhi kabhi darr lagta hai ki kahin humari yeh happiness hamesha na rahe."

He could feel the honesty in her words, the vulnerability that came from loving someone deeply. Taking a deep breath, he replied with all the reassurance he could give.

"Vannu, jitna humare haath mein hai, main kabhi kuch galat hone nahi dunga. Tum ho toh sab kuch theek hai. Yeh khushi humesha rahegi, I promise."

She sent a simple, *"Thank you, Shivu,"* and he could feel the warmth of her gratitude even through the screen. It was a reminder of the quiet strength they both found in each other—a love that grounded them, a connection that made everything feel possible.

That night, as they exchanged their usual *"Radhe Radhe, Good night, love you,"* Shivam lay awake, thinking about her words. He knew that the future was uncertain, but with Vanshika, he felt a strength he hadn't known before. And for now, that was enough.

The weeks rolled on, and with each passing day, Shivam found himself drawn deeper into the world he shared with Vanshika. She had become his source of joy, the person who could lift his spirits with a single message or a playful joke. Their connection felt unbreakable, and even the smallest conversations were laced with a warmth that made everything feel just right.

One evening, after they had spent hours talking about everything and nothing, Vanshika's message took on a softer tone.

"Shivu," she began, *"kabhi kabhi lagta hai ke tumhare saath saari zindagi bhi guzar jaye toh woh bhi kam padegi."*

Shivam's heart skipped a beat at her words. He took a moment to respond, wanting his reply to hold as much sincerity as her confession.

"Vannu, tum ho toh bas har lamha apne aap mein poora lagta hai. Tumhare saath hona is like finding something I didn't even know I was missing."

She sent back a heart emoji, and he could almost feel the gentle smile behind her words. Their conversations had a way of drifting into moments like these, where words became more than just words, and feelings flowed freely, unhindered by fear or doubt.

Just as they were about to end their conversation, Vanshika sent him a message that made him pause.

"Shivu, mere ghar walon ko ab kuch kuch shak ho raha hai... about us."

Shivam felt his stomach tighten at her words. Though he knew they couldn't keep their relationship a secret forever, he hadn't anticipated that the time would come so soon.

"Are you okay?" he asked, his tone immediately concerned. *"Agar tumhe kabhi bhi lagta hai ke main kuch help kar sakta hoon, you just have to say it."*

She replied with a soft reassurance. *"Haan, Shivu, I'm fine. Bas... thoda sa stress ho jata hai sometimes. Tum bas mere saath rehna, aur kuch nahi chahiye."*

Her words filled him with both relief and determination. He knew that their relationship would have its challenges, but he was ready to face them with her, no matter what.

As they ended the night with their usual *"Radhe Radhe, Good night, love you,"* Shivam felt a quiet resolve take root within him. Whatever came next, he knew they would face it together, and he would be there for her, just as she was for him.

As Shivam and Vanshika's relationship deepened, so did their playful exchanges, filled with nicknames, inside jokes, and phrases that had become uniquely theirs. Shivam loved finding ways to make her smile, and he often used her affectionate nickname, *"Madam ji,"* to add a bit of charm to their conversations.

One evening, as they chatted about their day, Vanshika teased him about his tendency to worry over the smallest things.

"You know, Shivu, kabhi kabhi tum bilkul old-fashioned lagte ho. Itni chinta toh mere parents bhi nahi karte," she laughed, adding a wink emoji.

"Oh ho, Madam ji," Shivam replied, grinning as he typed, *"agar main tumhara khayal nahi rakhunga toh aur kaun rakhega?"*

She sent back a playful eye-roll emoji, her message teasing. *"Arrey, mujhe apne aap kaafi sambhalna aata hai, Mr. Shivam."*

"Haan, haan, jaanta hoon," he replied, *"par fir bhi Madam ji ko thoda extra care dena mera farz hai, na?"*

Vanshika laughed, her reply carrying the warmth he loved. *"Alright, Shivu. Tumhe special permission mil gayi hai. Official care manager ban gaye ho."*

Shivam couldn't help but laugh, sending back a saluting emoji. *"Yes, Madam ji! Ab toh aapko khayal rakhne ka pura haq hai mere paas."*

Their conversation flowed easily, drifting from playful teasing to deeper thoughts and dreams. They spoke about their hopes, their plans, and the things they'd never shared with anyone else. Shivam loved these moments, the way they could go from laughter to vulnerability in the span of a few messages, each one bringing them closer.

Before they ended their chat that night, Vanshika's tone softened.

"Shivu, tumhe pata hai? Tumhare bina life bilkul incomplete lagti hai. It's like you've become a part of everything I do."

He felt a surge of emotion at her words, replying with equal sincerity. *"Vannu, tum mere liye woh ho jo bas life ko poora banati hai. Tum saath ho toh sab kuch sahi lagta hai."*

They closed the night, as they always did, with their familiar ritual: *"Radhe Radhe, Good night, love you."* And as Shivam lay in bed, he felt the happiness of knowing that they had found something rare and beautiful—something worth holding onto, no matter what lay ahead.

The days continued to pass in a haze of laughter and shared secrets. Shivam found himself growing more attached to Vanshika with every conversation, each interaction drawing them closer. Their playful banter had become a constant, with *"Madam ji"* and *"Mendak"* exchanges filling his evenings with warmth and joy.

One afternoon, as they talked about their dreams and passions, Vanshika casually mentioned, *"Waise, Shivu, tum writer ho, lekin kabhi tumne kuch apna likha hua nahi dikhaya. Are you sure you're as good as you say?"*

Shivam laughed, enjoying her challenge. *"Madam ji, aap shayad mere hidden talent ko underestimate kar rahi ho. Ek din padh ke toh dekho, fan ho jaogi."*

"Oh, really?" she replied with a laughing emoji. *"Then show me something, Mr. Writer. But don't get your hopes too high!"*

Shivam grinned, typing back, *"Madam ji ka hukum sir aankhon par. Kuch special likha hai tumhare liye. Dekhti jao!"*

He shared with her a few paragraphs from something he had written—a mix of poetry and storytelling that he'd poured his heart into. Vanshika responded almost instantly.

"Wow, Shivu! This is amazing! Mujhe sach mein nahi pata tha ke tum itna achha likhte ho."

"Told you, Madam ji," he replied with a wink. *"Aapne underestimate kiya tha apne mendak ko."*

"I admit, I was wrong," she wrote back, adding a heart. *"You really do have a way with words, Shivu."*

Her compliment lingered in his mind, filling him with quiet pride. It was as if Vanshika's appreciation had added a new meaning to his writing, making every word he'd crafted feel even more valuable.

As they wrapped up their conversation for the night, Shivam lay back, feeling a deep contentment. Vanshika had brought so much into his life—confidence, joy, and a sense of purpose that went beyond anything he'd known before. With her by his side, everything seemed possible.

Over time, Shivam's writing became a regular part of their conversations. Vanshika would eagerly read every piece he shared, often asking questions about his inspiration, what certain lines meant, and how he managed to capture emotions so vividly. For Shivam, these exchanges brought a sense of fulfillment he hadn't felt before; sharing his work with her made it all feel more meaningful.

One evening, as they talked about his latest piece, Vanshika messaged, *"Shivu, sach mein, tumhare words mein kuch alag hi magic hai. Pata nahi tum kaise itne emotions daal dete ho."*

Shivam felt his heart warm at her words. *"Madam ji, yeh toh aapka asar hai. Tumhari wajah se hi mere likhne mein aur depth aa gayi hai."*

She replied with a laughing emoji, her tone affectionate. *"Tumhare charm mein toh baatein banana bhi shamil hai, huh?"*

"Arrey, sach mein," he replied, grinning as he typed. *"Tum meri inspiration ho, aur tumhare liye likhne mein mujhe sabse zyada maza aata hai."*

Her response was instant and sincere, *"You know, Shivu, tumhara yeh talent mujhe aur bhi zyada proud feel karwata hai. Kabhi socha hai, tumhare words kitne logon tak pahunch sakte hain?"*

He paused, reflecting on her words. He'd always written as a personal outlet, never imagining that his work could impact others. But hearing her say it, Shivam felt a spark of motivation, a gentle push to consider sharing his writing beyond their private conversations.

"Mujhe kabhi yeh sochne ka mauka nahi mila, par agar tum kehti ho toh shayad kuch soch sakta hoon," he replied, feeling both nervous and excited.

"Good," she wrote back. *"Main tumhare har step mein tumhare saath hoon. Tumhare words deserve to be heard."*

Their conversation continued into the night, and for the first time, Shivam began to think seriously about taking his writing further. He drifted to sleep with the thought lingering, feeling a newfound sense of purpose. With Vanshika's unwavering support, he felt ready to explore possibilities he'd never considered before.

The days continued, filled with laughter, late-night chats, and small gestures that had become second nature between them. Shivam and Vanshika shared everything—their dreams, their fears, and all the little details that made up their everyday lives. Their relationship felt effortless, each conversation a reminder of the bond they shared.

One evening, as they were talking, Vanshika brought up a topic that caught Shivam by surprise.

"Shivu," she began slowly, *"kabhi kabhi lagta hai ke hum dono ke saath kitni misunderstandings ho sakti hain. Jaise agar kabhi koi aur humare beech mein aane ki koshish kare toh?"*

Shivam sensed the vulnerability in her words and replied carefully. *"Vannu, tum jaanti ho na humare beech kuch bhi aisa nahi hai jo kisi aur ke wajah se change ho sake. Tum par pura bharosa hai mujhe."*

She replied softly, *"Haan, par kabhi kabhi thoda sa darr lagta hai. Tum mere liye itne important ho gaye ho, Shivu. Bas yeh sochti hoon ke humesha aise hi rahe."*

Shivam felt a pang of emotion, her words a reminder of how deeply they both felt for each other. He typed back, *"Vannu, tumhe yeh sochne ki zaroorat bhi nahi hai. Tum aur main, hum dono ek dusre ke saath hain, aur bas yehi baat matter karti hai."*

There was a pause before she replied, her message carrying the relief he hoped she'd feel. *"Thank you, Shivu. Tumhare bina sab kuch ajeeb lagta hai."*

Their conversation shifted back to lighter topics, but Shivam couldn't shake the thought of what she'd said. He realized just how much Vanshika meant to him, that she had become an inseparable part of his world. She was the person he wanted to be there for, the one he wanted to see happy, no matter what it took.

As they ended their conversation for the night, Shivam found himself making a silent promise to her. Whatever happened, he would make sure their bond stayed strong, and he would always be there for her, just as she was for him.

As Shivam and Vanshika grew closer, Shivam found himself sharing more with the people he trusted, especially his friend Prince. Shivam had known Prince since school, and their friendship was built on years of shared experiences, trust, and countless inside jokes. Prince had a knack for making Shivam laugh, even on his hardest days, and he was one of the few people who knew about his relationship with Vanshika.

One evening, Shivam sent Prince a message, filling him in on the latest conversation he'd had with Vanshika.

"Bhai," Shivam wrote, *"kabhi kabhi lagta hai ki mere aur Vanshika ke beech bahut misunderstandings ho sakti hain. Woh kabhi kabhi insecure ho jaati hai."*

Prince replied instantly, his message filled with his usual humor. *"Arrey, bhai, yeh toh har relationship ka basic package hai. Thoda tension aur thoda pyaar ka mix."*

Shivam laughed, feeling a bit lighter. *"Sach keh raha hai, par kabhi kabhi lagta hai mujhe usse aur reassure karna chahiye."*

Prince's tone shifted to something more serious. *"Dekho, Shivam, jo tumhare dil mein hai woh tumhe bas directly bolna chahiye. Relationships mein clarity sabse zaroori hai."*

Shivam felt a quiet relief at his friend's words. Prince had a way of simplifying things, of making everything seem manageable, even when it felt overwhelming. *"Sahi keh raha hai, bhai. Bas usse yeh feel karwana hai ki main uske saath hoon, hamesha."*

"Exactly, bhai," Prince replied. *"Aur kabhi kuch zyada complicated lage toh apne bhai ko yaad rakhna!"*

Their conversation continued, filled with humor and advice, and Shivam felt grateful for Prince's presence in his life. Talking to him reminded Shivam of the importance of balance, of being there for Vanshika while also staying true to himself.

Later, when Shivam said goodnight to Vanshika, he felt a renewed sense of purpose, bolstered by the support he'd received from Prince. With friends like him, Shivam knew he was better equipped to face whatever challenges lay ahead.

Shivam's bond with Vasundhra was unique. She was more than just a friend; she was like a sister who could read him better than he could read himself. Whenever Shivam found himself overthinking or feeling uncertain, Vasundhra had a way of bringing him back to center, often with humor that left him both laughing and thinking.

One afternoon, as they exchanged messages, Vasundhra sent him a light-hearted nudge.

"Shivam," she wrote, *"kabhi kabhi lagta hai tum aur tumhare thoughts ka drama kabhi khatam nahi hota."* She added a laughing emoji, knowing he'd catch the joke.

Shivam laughed, typing back, *"Haan, madam, tumko toh mazak lagta hai. Lekin ye relationship ka tension asli hai!"*

She replied with her usual straightforwardness. *"Arrey, tension hai toh kya? Tumne kabhi socha hai ke itna overthink kyun karte ho? Tum bas apna best karo, baaki chhodo."*

Shivam felt a sense of relief at her words. There was something grounding about Vasundhra's practical way of looking at things, a reminder to enjoy the journey without focusing too much on every little worry. *"Sach kehti ho, Vasundhra. Tension lene ka kaam main hi karta hoon."*

"Exactly!" she replied with a grin emoji. *"Aur waise bhi, tum Vanshu ke liye perfect ho. Bas be yourself and don't overthink it."*

Her words were exactly what Shivam needed. It reminded him that, amidst everything, being himself was enough.

With friends like Vasundhra, he knew he'd always have someone to lean on, no matter what.

Over the next few days, Shivam noticed something that caught him off guard. Vanshika had started talking more frequently with Prince, messaging him during their group chats and sometimes mentioning their conversations to Shivam. At first, he brushed it off as a casual friendship, but as time went on, the pangs of jealousy began to creep in.

One evening, as they chatted, Vanshika casually mentioned, *"Prince was saying today that he might take up guitar lessons again. He's pretty good at it, you know."*

Shivam tried to keep his tone light as he replied, *"Oh, that's cool. I didn't know you guys were chatting about hobbies now."*

Vanshika laughed, adding a wink emoji. *"Arey, we talk about random stuff sometimes. He's actually pretty interesting, Shivu."*

Shivam felt a flicker of insecurity but quickly dismissed it, telling himself it was just a friendly conversation. But the feeling lingered, and over the next few days, he found himself overthinking every mention of Prince. Vanshika's laughter during group chats with Prince and her casual mentions of their conversations started to feel like small jabs, even if he knew it was all in his head.

Later that night, Shivam confided in Vasundhra, hoping her advice would help him see things clearly.

"*Vasundhra,*" he messaged, "*lagta hai main thoda overthink kar raha hoon, but it's weird seeing Vanshu talk with Prince so much. It just… bothers me.*"

Vasundhra replied almost immediately. "*Shivam, jealousy is normal. Bas apna confidence lose mat karo. Vanshu tumhare liye hai, aur Prince sirf ek dost hai. But I can talk to her if you want, just to clear things up.*"

Shivam hesitated but agreed. "*Maybe that's a good idea. I don't want to make it a big issue, but it's affecting me more than I thought it would.*"

Vasundhra reassured him, her message filled with the warmth he needed. "*I'll talk to her. Don't worry; I'll keep it light, but I'll make sure she understands.*"

With that, Shivam felt a little more at ease, trusting Vasundhra to handle the situation. He realized how deeply he valued his relationship with Vanshika and how much he wanted to keep it safe. As he closed his chat with Vasundhra, he resolved to trust Vanshika and stay true to himself.

The next day, Vasundhra reached out to Vanshika, approaching the conversation with a gentle touch. She knew how close Shivam and Vanshika were, and she wanted to make sure Vanshika understood the impact her actions were having on him, even if unintentionally.

"Hey, Vanshu," Vasundhra messaged, keeping her tone casual. *"Bas tumse ek baat share karni thi, hope you don't mind."*

Vanshika replied quickly, *"Of course not, Vasundhra! Kya baat hai?"*

Vasundhra chose her words carefully, typing, *"Tumhe pata hai na, Shivam tumhare liye kitna special feel karta hai. Kabhi kabhi woh Prince ke saath tumhari bonding dekh ke thoda insecure ho jata hai. It's nothing serious, but I just thought you should know."*

There was a pause before Vanshika responded, her tone thoughtful. *"Arrey, mujhe lagta tha woh bas mazak mein le raha hai. I didn't realize it was bothering him this much."*

Vasundhra smiled to herself, glad that Vanshika was understanding. *"Haan, woh bas chhupane ki koshish karta hai. Tum uske liye sab kuch ho, aur jab tum Prince ke saath thoda zyada friendly hoti ho, toh usko lagta hai ke tum uski feelings ko ignore kar rahi ho."*

Vanshika replied with a mix of surprise and regret. *"Oh, I feel bad now. I didn't mean to make him feel that way. Mujhe laga tha woh bas casually le raha hai, but I'll talk to him."*

Vasundhra's message was filled with reassurance. *"Don't worry, Vanshu. Tumhe bas ye dikhana hai ke tum uske saath ho. Shivam tum par pura bharosa karta hai, bas thoda attention chahiye usko."*

Later that evening, Vanshika messaged Shivam privately, her tone softer than usual.

"Shivu, tumne mujhe kabhi bataya nahi ki tum Prince ke saath meri baatein leke itne insecure ho rahe ho."

Shivam hesitated, unsure of how to respond. *"Mujhe laga tum notice nahi karogi, Vanshu. I didn't want to make it a big deal."*

She replied instantly, her words reassuring. *"Arrey, tum mere liye kitne important ho, tum samajhte kyun nahi? Prince bas ek dost hai, aur tum meri life ka woh hissa ho jise main kabhi nahi kho sakti."*

Shivam felt a wave of relief wash over him. *"Thank you, Vannu. Main bas tumhare saath honest rehna chahta hoon, and kabhi kabhi thoda possessive feel ho jata hoon."*

Vanshika sent back a heart emoji, her words filled with affection. *"It's okay, Shivu. I understand, and I'll make sure you never feel that way again."*

They ended the conversation with a sense of closeness that felt stronger than ever before, a reminder that their relationship could withstand the little challenges. For Shivam, this conversation was proof that, with trust and honesty, they could overcome anything.

The days were moving along as usual, but Shivam couldn't shake the feeling that something was different. Vanshika's messages felt a little shorter, her replies sometimes delayed, and there was a subtle shift in her tone. She still laughed at his jokes and replied with her usual affection, but he sensed an underlying tension that she hadn't shared with him yet.

One evening, as they were chatting, Shivam decided to bring it up.

"Vannu, sab theek hai na? You seem a bit... distracted lately. Kuch problem toh nahi hai?"

Vanshika's response came with a slight hesitation. *"Nahi, nahi, Shivu, sab theek hai. Bas thoda sa stressed hoon lately. Family stuff, you know."*

Shivam nodded, trying to respect her space. He didn't want to push, but he couldn't ignore the growing concern in his heart. *"Agar kuch bhi ho ya tumhe baat karni ho, you know I'm here, right?"*

She sent a small heart emoji in reply. *"Of course, Shivu. Tumhare saath baat karke sab kuch theek lagta hai."*

But even with her reassurances, Shivam couldn't shake the feeling that something bigger was happening. Vanshika was usually open with him about everything, and this sudden shift was unusual. He spent the next few days trying to be extra supportive, hoping it would help ease whatever was weighing on her mind.

Later, he shared his worries with Vasundhra, looking for advice.

"Vasundhra, mujhe lagta hai Vanshu kuch pareshaan hai, but she's not telling me. It feels like there's something big she's dealing with, but I don't want to push her."

Vasundhra replied with her usual straightforwardness. *"Give her some space, Shivam. Sometimes family issues take a while to sort out. She'll come to you when she's ready."*

Shivam nodded, appreciating her words but still feeling a pang of helplessness. He wanted to be there for Vanshika in every way possible, and the thought of her struggling alone weighed on him.

As the days passed, Shivam tried to remain patient, hoping she would eventually open up to him. Little did he know that this growing tension would soon lead to a moment that would change everything between them.

Shivam continued to notice Vanshika's subtle shifts in behavior. Her messages, once filled with warmth and excitement, now had moments of silence, replies that felt delayed, and a slight distance he couldn't ignore. He kept reminding himself of Vasundhra's advice to give her space, but the worry gnawed at him.

One afternoon, as they were chatting, Vanshika mentioned in passing, *"Aaj ghar mein thoda zyada strict environment hai, Shivu. Bas iss wajah se thoda low feel kar rahi hoon."*

Shivam's heart clenched. *"Koi specific wajah hai, Vannu? I mean, you seem really stressed."*

There was a pause before her reply came through. *"Kuch nahi, just family stuff. Main tumhe tension mein nahi dalna chahti, bas yeh samajh lo."*

Although he wanted to know more, Shivam sensed that pushing her for answers would only add to her stress. So, he decided to focus on lightening her mood instead, hoping it would bring some comfort.

"Thik hai, Madam ji," he teased, trying to keep things light. *"Lekin agar tumhe koi bhi help chahiye ya bas baat karna ho, remember I'm here."*

She sent back a heart emoji, her message reading, *"Pata hai, Shivu. Tumhare saath ho toh thoda sab kuch manageable lagta hai."*

Their conversation drifted to lighter topics, but Shivam could still sense a lingering tension. He didn't know that this small, seemingly harmless hint was leading to a much larger storm on the horizon—one that neither of them could prepare for.

As the day ended, Shivam's mind was filled with a mixture of worry and hope. He wanted to trust that everything would resolve itself, but deep down, he couldn't shake the feeling that they were on the edge of something life-altering.

The tension between Shivam and Vanshika continued to simmer beneath the surface, and although their chats were still filled with the same warmth and affection, Shivam could feel an invisible wall forming. Vanshika's responses remained caring, but her usual spark was dimmed, weighed down by something she wasn't ready to reveal.

One evening, as they were chatting, Vanshika's message came through with a more serious tone.

"Shivu," she began, *"kya tum kabhi feel karte ho ke humare relationship ke wajah se life thodi complicated ho gayi hai?"*

Shivam's heart skipped a beat. He took a deep breath before responding, trying to choose his words carefully. *"Mujhe aisa nahi lagta, Vannu. Tumhare saath hone se toh sab kuch aur simple aur meaningful ho gaya hai."*

There was a long pause before she replied, *"Haan, mujhe bhi yahi feel hota hai… par kabhi kabhi lagta hai, agar family ko pata chala toh kya hoga?"*

Shivam's pulse quickened. He hadn't realized how much the weight of her family's expectations was affecting her. *"Dekho, jo bhi ho, hum saath hain. Tumhe kabhi yeh relationship ke wajah se kuch difficult lage toh mujhe bata sakti ho."*

"Thanks, Shivu," she replied softly. *"Main bas thodi si dar gayi hoon. Lekin tumhare saath baat karke thoda better feel ho raha hai."*

They continued talking, drifting back into lighter topics, but Shivam's mind remained on her words. This fear she had of her family finding out was something he couldn't easily dismiss. It was a reminder of the delicate balance they had to maintain, where one wrong step could lead to consequences they couldn't control.

As they ended their conversation for the night, Shivam lay in bed, his thoughts racing. He wanted to believe that love could conquer anything, but he knew that life wasn't always so simple. With a quiet resolve, he promised himself that he'd be there for her, no matter what lay ahead.

The unease between them continued to grow, each passing day bringing more hints of Vanshika's internal struggle. Shivam sensed her worries were becoming harder for her to keep hidden, and he felt increasingly helpless, watching her slowly drift into a world of anxiety that he couldn't seem to penetrate.

One evening, as they chatted, Vanshika's words held a heaviness that was hard to ignore.

"Shivu," she typed, her tone serious, *"kabhi kabhi lagta hai ki family expectations aur hamari relationship ke beech mein ek constant tension hai."*

Shivam responded carefully, wanting to be supportive without pressuring her to share more than she was comfortable with. *"Vannu, main samajhta hoon ke tumhare liye family kitna important hai. Par tumhe yaad hai na, jo bhi ho, hum isme saath hain?"*

There was a pause before she replied, her words honest and vulnerable. *"I know, Shivu. Lekin kabhi kabhi darr lagta hai. Agar kabhi kuch aisa ho jaye jo humare control mein nahi ho, toh kya hoga?"*

Shivam felt his heart sink. He had always known that family expectations weighed heavily on Vanshika, but hearing her express this fear so directly made him realize the depth of her worry. *"Dekho, jo bhi ho, main tumhare saath hoon. Tumhe apni family ke decisions aur unki khushiyon ka bhi dhyaan rakhna hai, par apne liye bhi sochna hai."*

She sent back a small heart emoji, her reply soft. *"Thanks, Shivu. Tum ho toh sab manageable lagta hai."*

But even with her words of gratitude, Shivam knew that this was a battle he couldn't fight for her. All he could do was stand by her, hoping that their bond would be strong enough to endure whatever came their way.

As they said goodnight, Shivam felt the weight of uncertainty settle over him. He knew that a storm was on the horizon, and all they could do was brace themselves for whatever lay ahead.

The Revelation

The tension between Shivam and Vanshika had reached a new high, but neither of them could have anticipated what was coming next. One evening, Vanshika messaged Shivam, her words coming through with an unusual urgency.

"Shivu," she typed, *"kuch serious baat karni hai."*

Shivam's heart skipped a beat as he read her message. *"Kya hua, Vannu? Tum itni tense kyun ho?"*

She replied, her message short and clipped. *"Deepanshi ko uske dad ne uske boyfriend ke saath dekh liya. Bahut badi problem ho gayi hai ghar pe."*

Shivam felt a wave of dread wash over him. He knew how strict Deepanshi's family could be and understood the consequences she might face. But what he hadn't anticipated was the ripple effect this incident would soon have on his own life.

Before he could respond, Vanshika's next message came through.

"Aur iss sab mein, usne unko humare baare mein bhi bata diya."

The ground seemed to shift beneath Shivam's feet as he read her words. This was something they had always feared—a moment when their private world would be exposed, leading to consequences neither of them were ready for.

"Kya?" Shivam replied, his fingers trembling slightly. *"Tumhare parents ko bhi sab kuch pata chal gaya?"*

Vanshika's reply came through with an air of resignation. *"Haan, Shivu. Unhone mujhse poori baat poochhi, aur mujhe sach batana pada. Ab woh mujhpar aur tum par gussa hain."*

Shivam felt his heart sink, realizing the magnitude of the situation. Vanshika's family had always been her first priority, and he knew how hard it must have been for her to deal with their anger and disappointment.

As he processed her words, he could sense that this was only the beginning of a difficult journey for both of them.

Shivam's mind raced as he tried to make sense of Vanshika's words. He could only imagine the shock and anger her parents must have felt. Vanshika messaged him again, her tone revealing the weight of her distress.

"Shivu, unka reaction… woh bahut hi zyada emotional aur hurt ho gaye. Unhone kaha ki unhone kabhi aisa expect nahi kiya tha."

Shivam felt a wave of empathy for her, but he also knew there was little he could do from where he was. *"Vannu, tum bas unko samjhane ki koshish karo. Unhe time lagega, lekin shayad woh baat ko samajh lenge."*

Her next message showed just how difficult things had become. *"Nahi, Shivu. Unhone mujhe tumse baat karna bilkul mana kar diya hai. Mere mom ne kaha hai ke agar maine tumse phir se baat ki toh unke liye woh meri kasam hogi."*

Shivam's heart sank. He knew Vanshika's parents held deep values, and such a strong statement left little room for compromise. The thought of not speaking to her, not sharing the small details of their day, seemed almost unbearable.

"Toh ab kya karoge, Vannu?" he typed, his fingers heavy.

"Mujhe nahi pata, Shivu," she replied, the pain in her words palpable. *"Main tumhe nahi khona chahti, lekin family bhi mere liye sab kuch hai."*

They both fell silent, Shivam struggling with the helplessness of the situation. He knew that Vanshika was caught between the love they shared and the loyalty she felt for her family, a position that forced her to choose between two equally important parts of her life.

After a few moments, he finally replied, *"Vannu, agar tumhe apne family ke liye thodi doori banani padti hai, toh main samajhta hoon. Main yahi chahta hoon ke tum khush raho, chahe tumhare saath ya door se."*

Her response came through with a quiet gratitude that broke his heart. *"Thank you, Shivu. Tum sach mein samajh rahe ho, aur mujhe yeh bahut important hai."*

They ended the conversation that night with an understanding that, for now, they had to create some distance. Shivam lay awake, feeling the weight of a loss that hadn't fully happened yet but felt inevitable.

The next few days passed in a haze of silence and uncertainty. Vanshika and Shivam had agreed to keep some distance, but the ache of separation felt almost unbearable. Shivam found himself checking his phone constantly, hoping for a message from her, even if he knew it was unlikely. It was as if every quiet moment reminded him of her absence, each passing day intensifying the void she'd left behind.

One evening, he finally received a message from her. The notification brought a momentary spark of joy, but as he opened it, her words hit him with the gravity of their reality.

"Shivu, I'm so sorry. Mujhe pata hai ke tum bhi yeh distance se struggle kar rahe ho, lekin mujhe apne gharwalon ko bhi samay dena padega. Unka trust dobara jeetna hai."

He understood, but the understanding didn't lessen the pain. *"Main samajhta hoon, Vannu. Tum apne family ke saath ho, aur tumhara unka trust wapas paana zaroori hai. Lekin tumhe yeh bhi pata hai na, ke main tumhara intezaar karunga."*

There was a pause before her response came. *"I know, Shivu. Tumhare intezaar ke liye hi toh yeh sab thoda easy lagta hai."*

Shivam held onto those words, feeling the reassurance they provided. Even if they couldn't be together right now, knowing that Vanshika still held him close in her heart gave him strength. But he also sensed the sadness in her words, a subtle acknowledgment that neither of them knew how long this separation would last.

As the days turned into weeks, Shivam leaned on his closest friends, especially Vasundhra and Sujal. They became his pillars of strength, encouraging him to stay hopeful, even when the path seemed uncertain.

One evening, as he shared his thoughts with Vasundhra and Sujal, he expressed the heaviness he felt. *"Kabhi kabhi lagta hai ki yeh intezaar mushkil hai, par main apne pyaar par bharosa rakhta hoon."*

Vasundhra replied with her usual straightforwardness. *"Shivam, agar tumhara pyaar sachha hai, toh yeh waqt bhi guzar jayega. Bas thoda patience aur faith rakhna padega."*

Sujal added, *"Aur hum tumhare saath hain, bhai. Jab bhi lage ke yeh sab tough ho raha hai, yaad rakhna ke hum yahan hain."*

Their words brought Shivam a sense of resilience he hadn't realized he needed. With Vasundhra and Sujal by his side, he found a quiet strength, reminding himself that he could wait, no matter how long it took, until the day he and Vanshika could be together once again.

Shivam's life settled into a new rhythm, one that revolved around waiting, hoping, and relying on the quiet strength of his friends. Every day felt like a test of patience, and while he missed Vanshika deeply, he found solace in knowing that their love was still strong, even from a distance. Vasundhra and Sujal became his steady anchors, their presence reminding him that he wasn't alone in this journey.

One evening, after a particularly challenging day, Shivam met with Sujal for a walk. As they strolled down the familiar lanes, Sujal broke the silence.

"Bhai," Sujal began, his tone serious yet comforting, *"kabhi kabhi yeh sab asaan nahi hota, but I can see that you're handling it well. Tumhare liye yeh intezaar ka safar sach mein kitna mushkil hai."*

Shivam nodded, grateful for his friend's understanding. *"Sujal, kabhi kabhi lagta hai ke yeh sab bas ek khwab hai jo kabhi pura nahi hoga. Lekin jab uske saath guzare hue pal yaad aate hain, toh woh yaadein mujhe sab kuch sehne ki taqat deti hain."*

Sujal smiled, patting Shivam on the shoulder. *"Yahi toh asli pyaar hai, bhai. Agar tumhare dil mein itna saccha pyaar hai, toh yeh intezaar bhi worth lagta hai."*

Later that night, Vasundhra messaged him, checking in as she often did. She had an uncanny ability to sense when Shivam was feeling low, and her timing was always perfect.

"Shivam, remember that waiting doesn't mean you're losing anything," she wrote. *"You're just holding onto something that's worth every second of this wait."*

Shivam replied with a quiet gratitude, *"Thank you, Vasundhra. Tum dono ke bina yeh sab shayad main itna strongly face nahi kar paata."*

Vasundhra replied with a simple heart, her support tangible through the screen. *"We're here for you, Shivam. Tum kabhi bhi akela feel mat karna."*

In those moments, Shivam realized that while he was waiting for the day he could be with Vanshika, he was surrounded by a love and friendship that made him stronger. With Vasundhra and Sujal by his side, he found a renewed sense of hope, ready to face whatever lay ahead with quiet resilience.

Days turned into weeks, and Shivam's life became a balancing act of hope and resilience. He tried to keep himself occupied, immersing himself in his studies, spending time with friends, and doing everything he could to keep the ache of separation at bay. Still, every time his phone buzzed, his heart leapt, hoping it would be a message from Vanshika.

One evening, as he was sitting with Vasundhra and Sujal at a small cafe they often visited, Shivam shared his thoughts openly, his guard finally dropping.

"Kabhi kabhi lagta hai ki Vanshu ka intezaar mere se nahi hoga," he admitted, his voice low. *"Yeh sab waqt aur doori... bahut mushkil hai."*

Vasundhra looked at him, her expression a mixture of understanding and encouragement. *"Shivam, itna asaan nahi hai, par tum dono ke beech ka connection bahut special hai. Agar tum yeh waqt paar kar sakte ho, toh tum dono ka pyaar aur bhi gehra ho jayega."*

Sujal added, nodding in agreement, *"Aur bhai, kabhi kabhi intezaar hi pyaar ki asli pariksha hoti hai. Bas apna bharosa banaye rakh, aur jo bhi ho, hum tere saath hain."*

Their words gave Shivam a momentary comfort, reminding him of the strength he had within himself and the people around him. He realized that this waiting wasn't just about distance but about the lessons it taught him—about patience, trust, and the true meaning of love.

Later that night, Shivam sat alone in his room, scrolling through his past messages with Vanshika, reliving their happiest moments together. The memories flooded him, bringing both a smile and a deep ache to his heart. In one of their messages, he had promised her that no matter the distance or the challenges, he would always be there.

"Yeh waqt bhi guzar jayega," he whispered to himself, his voice filled with quiet determination. *"Aur jab woh wapas aayegi, hum dono ke beech ka pyaar aur bhi mazboot ho jayega."*

With that thought, Shivam found a renewed sense of peace, holding onto the love he shared with Vanshika as his guiding light. He knew the path ahead would be challenging, but he was ready, for her and for the love that had come to define his life.

Lingering Longing and Reality

Shivam's days felt quieter now, as if the silence around him had taken on a life of its own. Vanshika's absence echoed in every part of his day, and while he tried to adjust, it was hard to ignore the empty space she'd left. He kept himself busy, filling his time with studies and meeting friends, but the quiet longing remained, especially in the late hours when memories felt the sharpest.

One evening, as he scrolled through his old messages with Vanshika, a familiar ache returned. It was a mix of joy and pain, remembering the warmth they had shared, and he found himself typing out a message before he could stop.

"Hey Vannu, hope you're doing well. Bas tumhe yaad kar raha tha."

He stared at the screen, wondering if she'd respond. Moments stretched into minutes, and finally, her message appeared.

"Hey, Shivu... I'm okay. Just really busy these days."

The words felt distant, as if an invisible wall had formed between them. Her response, though polite, lacked the spark that used to light up their conversations. Shivam typed back, trying to keep things light.

"I understand. Bas tumhari yaad aa gayi thi. Tumhare bina life thoda ajeeb lagta hai."

After a long pause, she replied with a simple, *"I miss those days too, Shivu."*

Reading her words, Shivam felt a momentary relief, but he could sense her hesitation, as if there was something unspoken in the silence that followed. He knew she was trying to balance the weight of her family's expectations and the bond they had once shared, and it pained him to see her so torn.

Later that night, he poured his emotions into a *shayari* that captured the bittersweet nature of his feelings.

"Woh lamhe yaad hai, jo hamesha apne the,
Ab dooriyan hain, par ehsaas wohi apne hai."

Writing became his solace, a way to keep their memories alive, even as reality drifted them further apart. It was the one thing that made the ache bearable, giving him a place to express the depth of his longing for her, no matter how far away she seemed.

As days turned into weeks, Shivam found himself clinging to the small moments he still shared with Vanshika. Though their conversations were infrequent and brief, each word from her felt like a lifeline. He tried to keep his messages light, hoping to reignite some of the closeness they once had, but there was always a subtle distance in her replies, a reminder that things had changed.

One evening, he shared his thoughts with Vasundhra over a call, hoping she could offer some clarity.

"Vasundhra, yeh jo silsila hai... is distance ka, it's tearing me apart. Bas uske saath wahi connection wapas paane ki koshish kar raha hoon, lekin woh jaise door hoti ja rahi hai."

Vasundhra's voice softened, filled with understanding. *"Shivam, sometimes holding onto someone means letting them breathe. Tum uske liye important ho, yeh woh bhi jaanti hai. But maybe this distance is her way of coping with all the pressure around her."*

Shivam listened, realizing that Vasundhra was right. Vanshika had always been close to her family, and he knew how much she valued their happiness. It wasn't easy for her to be caught between two worlds, and as much as it hurt him, he had to respect her process.

That night, he opened his notebook and let the emotions flow, his pen moving almost unconsciously as he wrote a *shayari* that captured the essence of his heartache.

"Tumse door reh kar bhi paas rehne ki koshish karte hain,
Har shab tumhari yaadon mein hum khud se guftagu karte
hain."

He stared at the words, feeling a wave of bittersweet
satisfaction. Writing allowed him to stay connected to her
in his own way, each verse an extension of his love that
went beyond the boundaries of distance.

In those quiet moments, he realized that while the reality of
their separation was painful, his love for her had taken on a
new form. It was no longer just about their shared
moments, but about the lessons she had left with him,
lessons he carried with every word he wrote.

The separation lingered, and Shivam found himself caught in an endless loop of memories and hopes. Each day, he revisited moments they had shared, finding comfort in those memories even as they pulled him deeper into longing. He spent his nights writing, pouring his emotions onto the page as a way to keep his connection with Vanshika alive, even if only in spirit.

One afternoon, he received a message from a mutual friend, Sanjana, who shared occasional updates about Vanshika. Her words were simple, but they carried a weight that struck Shivam unexpectedly.

"Vanshu has been busy with family things lately. She's trying to move forward, but she asks about you sometimes."

Shivam read and reread the message, his heart a mix of relief and sadness. Knowing she still thought about him provided some comfort, but the reality that she was attempting to move on made him feel as though he was slowly losing her all over again.

That evening, he shared his thoughts with Sujal, who had been a steady source of support through it all.

"Sujal, kabhi kabhi lagta hai ke Vanshu sach mein door ja rahi hai," Shivam confided, his voice heavy with resignation. *"Lekin phir bhi mann yeh nahi maanta ki woh mujhe poori tarah se bhool payegi."*

Sujal listened intently before replying, *"Yaar, pyaar ka yeh ek ajeeb sa aspect hai. Kabhi kabhi, letting go is the hardest but most genuine act of love. Agar tumhaare dil*

*mein woh hamesha zinda rahegi, toh shayad tumhe woh
poori tarah se kabhi chhod ke ja hi nahi sakti."*

Shivam nodded, the weight of Sujal's words settling over
him. Perhaps this was the reality he had to accept—holding
onto his memories of her, without expecting anything more.

Later that night, he picked up his notebook once again, his
pen moving almost instinctively as he expressed the
bittersweet ache of his love.

*"Yeh dooriyan toh bas faasla hai humare darmiyaan,
Tum mere dil mein ho, yeh fasana hai humare beech ka
asar."*

In that quiet moment, he made peace with the idea that
some stories live on, even if they don't have a clear ending.
His love for Vanshika was one such story, written in words
that only he would truly understand.

The Pain of Letting Go

For a long moment, Shivam sat there, reading and rereading Sanjana's message. The thought of Vanshika moving on, especially with someone else, was like a knife twisting in his chest. He tried to convince himself it was just a rumor, a baseless piece of gossip that didn't mean anything. But even as he told himself this, an ache settled deep within him, refusing to be ignored.

After a few minutes, Shivam replied to Sanjana, his words hesitant.

"Sanjana, are you sure about this? Maybe it's just people talking."

Sanjana's response came quickly. *"I know it's hard to hear, Shivam. But I thought it was better you know. Vanshika hasn't said anything directly, but there's talk that she might be seeing someone named Prateek. Maybe it's her way of moving forward."*

Shivam's heart sank as he read her words. He wanted to brush it off as just a misunderstanding, a product of someone else's assumptions. But somewhere deep down, he knew there was a chance that Vanshika, faced with her family's expectations, might actually be moving on.

Sanjana's words echoed in his mind long after their conversation ended, leaving him with a bitter sense of loss and helplessness. It felt as if all the hope he'd been clinging to was slipping through his fingers, forcing him to confront the reality he had been trying so hard to avoid.

That night, Shivam turned to his notebook, letting his feelings flow into words. His *shayari* captured the pain of watching someone he loved slip away, even if only in rumors.

"Usne shayad naya raasta dhoondh liya hai,
Aur main uske qadmon ke nishaan mein reh gaya hoon kho gaya hoon."

As he closed his notebook, Shivam felt a mixture of sadness and acceptance. Maybe it was time to truly let go, to accept that some stories, no matter how beautiful, don't always have a second chapter.

The news about Prateek weighed heavily on Shivam in the days that followed. He found himself questioning everything, replaying moments with Vanshika and wondering if he had missed signs of her moving on. Though he tried to stay calm, his thoughts constantly returned to the possibility that she might be with someone else, and each time, the thought felt like a fresh wound.

One evening, as he sat alone in his room, Shivam couldn't help but reach for his phone, instinctively scrolling through old messages with Vanshika. Reading through their conversations, he felt a bittersweet nostalgia—a reminder of everything they had shared and a stark contrast to the silence that had grown between them.

He knew he couldn't change the circumstances or make her decisions for her. But the ache of letting go of someone he loved so deeply left him feeling hollow. Seeking some form of release, he picked up his notebook and started writing, his words a reflection of the pain that seemed to have no end.

"Uske bina bhi zindagi chal rahi hai, par woh raunak gayi hai,
Dil mein ab bhi woh bas gayi hai, par khamoshi se baatein ho rahi hai."

The *shayari* brought him a momentary relief, but it couldn't mask the lingering sadness that hung in the air. He felt like he was caught between holding onto memories and trying to move forward, unsure which path would bring him peace.

That night, he messaged Sujal, needing the support of a friend who understood the depths of his heartache.

"Bhai, kabhi kabhi lagta hai sab kuch chhod kar aage badhne ka waqt aa gaya hai," Shivam typed, feeling the weight of each word. *"Par phir uski yaadein aane lagti hain, aur main wahi atak jata hoon."*

Sujal's reply was quick and understanding. *"Shivam, letting go doesn't mean you have to erase her. Woh tumhare saath hamesha ek yaad banke rahegi. Shayad ab tumhe apni khushi uske bina dhoondhne ka waqt aa gaya hai."*

As Shivam read Sujal's message, he realized that maybe Sujal was right. Vanshika might always remain a cherished memory, a beautiful chapter in his life, but he had to find his way forward, carrying her presence with him rather than being trapped by it.

In the days that followed, Shivam clung to a delicate balance between his memories and the quiet realization that he needed to find peace, even if it meant moving forward alone. Vanshika's presence lingered like a familiar scent, her absence more real with each passing moment. Yet, Shivam knew that he couldn't hold onto someone who wasn't fully with him anymore, no matter how deeply he still cared.

To cope, he threw himself into writing, finding solace in every line of *shayari* that allowed him to express the ache he carried. His words became his only companion in the silence, capturing the depth of his longing and the bittersweet beauty of a love that had become a memory.

"Teri yaadon mein jee rahe hain ab,
Woh pal jo the humare, unhi mein kho rahe hain ab."

The *shayari* flowed effortlessly, each line an echo of the love he couldn't let go of completely. As he shared some of his writing with Vasundhra, she encouraged him, seeing how it was helping him to process his feelings.

One afternoon, as they sat together over coffee, Vasundhra looked at him thoughtfully.

"Shivam, tumhari shayari mein itni gehrai hai, it's like you're pouring your heart into every word," she said gently. *"Shayad yeh waqt tumhe bas apne aap ko aur explore karne ka hai."*

Shivam smiled, though it didn't quite reach his eyes.
*"Haan, Vasundhra. Shayari toh bas ek raasta hai uss sab ko
bayaan karne ka, jo main bol nahi paata."*

She nodded, her expression empathetic. *"Aur wohi tumhari
taqat hai. Tum apne emotions ko aise express kar sakte ho
jo bohot log nahi kar paate. Tumhe yeh talent kisi wajah se
mila hai, Shivam."*

Her words resonated with him, giving him a glimpse of
purpose he hadn't considered before. Maybe his
experiences with Vanshika—the love, the longing, the
heartbreak—were shaping him in ways he hadn't yet
realized. Perhaps, in a way, this journey was meant to help
him find his voice, one that could speak not only of his own
feelings but of emotions that others, too, might share.

Later that night, Shivam wrote in his notebook, letting his
words capture the strange, transformative power of love.

*"Woh yaadon mein toh rahegi, par uska ehsaas ab khud se
hai,
Pyaar jo usne diya, woh mere har lafz mein zinda hai."*

For the first time, Shivam felt a small sense of closure. His
love for Vanshika was now etched into every line he wrote,
a part of him that would live on, even as he learned to let
go.

A few days after their last conversation, Sanjana messaged Shivam again, her tone more hesitant this time.

"Shivam, there's something I need to tell you about that Prateek thing," she started, her words leaving him anxious.

"What is it, Sanjana?" he replied, feeling a mix of curiosity and dread.

There was a slight pause before her message came through. *"Vanshika told me that… well, it was all a prank. She just wanted me to believe she was moving on so that I'd tell you and discourage you from holding onto her."*

Shivam sat there, stunned, rereading her words. A prank? The idea left him feeling a mixture of relief, confusion, and frustration. He had spent days grappling with the thought of losing Vanshika to someone else, only to realize that it was all an attempt to push him away. For a moment, he didn't know whether to feel grateful or angry.

"Why would she do that?" he typed, the question more to himself than to Sanjana. His heart felt heavy with the realization that Vanshika had gone to such lengths to create distance between them.

Sanjana's reply was cautious. *"I think she wants you to stop waiting for her, Shivam. She cares about you, but maybe she thinks this is the only way to help you let go."*

Shivam felt his heart tighten. He understood her intentions, but the pain was still real. It was as if she had taken away the last bit of hope he had been holding onto, forcing him to confront the reality of their separation in a way he hadn't been ready for.

That night, he sat alone, feeling the weight of the situation sink in. The prank, though harmless in appearance, had brought a deeper sense of finality to their relationship, one he hadn't expected.

Later, he opened his notebook, his emotions spilling out in a few quiet words.

"Usne door jaane ka ek naya bahaana bana diya,
Par main toh ab bhi uske intezaar mein khoya hu."

The line captured the bittersweet truth he couldn't escape: he was still waiting, still hoping, even if it meant holding on to something that was slipping away.

The realization that Vanshika had orchestrated the prank lingered in Shivam's mind, filling him with a complicated mixture of relief, frustration, and heartbreak. It was clear that she was trying to push him away deliberately, hoping he'd let go. Yet, despite her efforts, he found himself unable to sever the connection he felt with her.

He spent the evening replaying old memories, recalling every smile, every shared laugh, and every moment that had defined their bond. It was hard to accept that these memories, once a source of happiness, now served as a painful reminder of everything he had lost.

Just as he was drowning in his thoughts, a message popped up on his screen. It was from Vanshika.

"Shivam, I know you heard about Prateek. And I know it must have hurt, but it was necessary. I don't want you waiting for me anymore."

Her words felt cold, final. He wanted to reply, to tell her that he didn't care about the prank, that he was willing to wait, but she continued typing before he could respond.

"I've moved on, Shivam. You need to do the same. Please let go. This... this is the end."

The message was like a knife to his heart. He stared at the screen, his fingers frozen over the keyboard as he struggled to find the right words to reply. But what could he say? Vanshika's decision was clear, and for the first time, he felt the weight of her absence pressing down on him.

His hands trembled as he finally typed out a response. *"If that's what you want, Vanshika, I'll respect your wishes. But remember, my feelings won't change overnight."*

With that, he closed the chat, feeling a hollow emptiness settle within him. That night, he wrote one last line in his notebook, capturing the ache that had now become a part of him.

"Woh door gayi hai, par mere dil mein uska asar hamesha zinda rahega."

He knew he couldn't keep waiting for her, but letting go would be a journey all its own.

Shivam tried to let her final words sink in, but the pain refused to fade. Vanshika's message was clear, and though he wanted to respect her wishes, his heart wasn't ready to simply erase the feelings he'd held onto for so long. The days that followed felt empty, as if the world around him had dulled in her absence.

He kept replaying their last conversation in his mind, the tone of her words, the finality of it all. It was difficult to accept, but he knew he had to start moving forward, even if it meant carrying her memory without expecting anything more.

In an attempt to fill the silence, Shivam leaned on his friendships with Vasundhra and Sujal, both of whom became his pillars of strength through the heartache. One evening, he met them at their usual spot, a small café that had become a place of comfort over the years.

Vasundhra gave him a concerned look as they sat down. *"Shivam, tumhe dekh kar lagta hai ke tum andar hi andar ab bhi uska intezaar kar rahe ho."*

Shivam forced a smile, trying to reassure her. *"Mujhe pata hai, Vasundhra. Par dil hai na… woh bas haar maan hi nahi raha."*

Sujal placed a hand on his shoulder. *"Bhai, pyaar toh hamesha saath rahega. Par shayad ab tumhe apne khud ke liye aage badhna padega. Waqt ke saath shayad dard kam ho jaaye."*

Shivam nodded, knowing they were right. He had to begin finding his own peace, even if it meant accepting that Vanshika would forever be a part of his past, not his present.

That night, as he walked home alone, Shivam felt a strange sense of calm settle over him. It wasn't the relief he had once hoped for, but it was a start—a quiet acceptance of the love he would always carry, even if it was no longer reciprocated.

"Mujhe uske bina jeena seekhna padega, par uski yaad mein kho jaana bhi zaroori hai," he whispered to himself, feeling a bittersweet resolve form within him.

He wasn't sure what the future held, but for now, he knew he would honor her memory without letting it consume him.

As Shivam worked through the ache of letting go, he remembered a small gift he had picked up for Vanshika during a recent trip to Jaipur. He'd chosen it with care, thinking of her smile when she'd receive it, unaware that their relationship would soon take this painful turn.

Now, the thought of giving her the gift felt bittersweet. Still, he couldn't bring himself to abandon it entirely, so he reached out to Sanjana, hoping she would help him.

"Sanjana, yeh gift Vanshika ke liye hai. Main Jaipur se laya tha... par ab usse khud nahi de paunga," he messaged her, feeling the weight of his decision.

Sanjana replied with understanding. *"Don't worry, Shivam. Main us tak pohncha dungi."*

A few days later, Sanjana confirmed that she had given Vanshika the gift. Shivam didn't expect anything in return, but just knowing that Vanshika had received it brought him a small sense of closure. It was his final gesture, a quiet acknowledgment of everything they had shared.

As he reflected on this, Shivam felt a calmness he hadn't experienced before. Letting go wasn't easy, but this small act allowed him to feel as though he had honored his feelings for her in a way that didn't demand anything in return.

With a deep breath, he knew it was time to move forward—gently, without rushing, allowing himself to heal in his own way.

"Ab bas yaadon ka ek silsila reh gaya hai,
Woh toh door chali gayi, par uska ehsaas mere paas reh
gaya hai."

And with that, Shivam began to close a chapter in his life, accepting that while he would always love her, he had to find peace on his own.

Shivam moved through his days quietly, the routines of life giving him a sense of stability, even though his heart remained anchored in memories of Vanshika. She was gone, and yet, she was everywhere—her laughter in the corners of his mind, her warmth in the small spaces of silence. Despite her request for him to move on, he couldn't bring himself to let go entirely.

Every now and then, he found himself wondering if she might come back. It was a small, stubborn hope, a quiet vigil he held within himself, waiting patiently, even if no one else understood why.

One evening, Vasundhra and Sujal joined him for a walk, their presence bringing him comfort as they strolled down the familiar streets. Though Shivam kept his thoughts to himself, Vasundhra sensed his lingering emotions.

"Shivam," she began softly, *"tum ab bhi uska intezaar kar rahe ho, nahi?"*

He paused, looking at her with a mixture of vulnerability and quiet strength. *"Haan, Vasundhra,"* he admitted. *"Woh toh apni raah chal gayi, lekin mera dil uska intezaar karna nahi bhoolta. Shayad kabhi bhool hi nahi payega."*

Sujal placed a reassuring hand on Shivam's shoulder, his voice gentle but understanding. *"Bhai, kabhi kabhi pyaar ka matlab sirf paas rehna nahi hota. Shayad yeh waqt tumhare liye ek alag tarah ka safar hai, par hum tumhare saath hain."*

Shivam nodded, grateful for their support. They didn't question his decision to wait, didn't ask him to forget her. Their quiet understanding was enough, allowing him to hold onto his hope without judgment.

Later that night, alone in his room, Shivam wrote a few lines in his notebook, expressing the gentle but persistent ache that had become his constant companion.

"Uske intezaar mein hi meri zindagi hai,
Woh aaye ya na aaye, yeh dil toh uska rahega."

As he closed the notebook, he felt a sense of peace settle over him. Waiting for her was no longer just a choice; it was a part of who he was, a quiet promise he held close to his heart.

And even if she never returned, he knew that his love for her would remain, an unwavering light in the silence.

The Silent Vigil

As months passed, Shivam held onto his memories of Vanshika, even as her absence became a part of his everyday life. He didn't wait for her messages or search for her in crowded places anymore, but the feeling of her presence remained, woven into quiet moments and familiar routines. Her memory had become something he held close, even if he no longer expected her return.

One afternoon, hoping for a small piece of news, he messaged Sanjana.

"Have you heard from Vanshika recently?" he typed carefully, bracing himself.

Sanjana responded with a gentle honesty. *"Shivam, she's doing well, busy with her studies and family. She's... moving forward. I just hope you can find peace too, in your own way."*

Shivam read her words, feeling a bittersweet ache. He knew Vanshika had let go, just as she'd told him, but his feelings hadn't diminished. They had simply become a quiet part of him, something he no longer expected anyone else to understand.

Later that evening, he met with Vasundhra, who had noticed the calm resolve he'd developed over the months.

"You seem... different, Shivam," she observed, studying his expression carefully.

He smiled faintly, feeling a mix of sadness and acceptance. *"I think I am, Vasundhra. I'm not waiting in the same way anymore... but uski yaadon mein reh kar hi jeene ka ek naya tareeka dhoondh liya hai."*

Vasundhra reached out, placing a comforting hand on his shoulder. *"Sometimes, carrying those memories with peace is its own kind of strength. Maybe she's not here, but you're keeping her in a way that's meaningful to you."*

That night, as he walked home, Shivam felt a quiet calm settle over him. His love for Vanshika had changed shape—it was no longer bound to hope or expectation, but to a deep gratitude for what they had shared.

*"Intezaar mein bhi ek sukoon hai,
Woh aaye na aaye, par uska ehsaas hamesha saath hai."*

And with that acceptance, Shivam found a sense of peace, embracing his love for Vanshika as a part of himself that he would always carry forward.

With each passing month, Shivam learned to live with the
ache that came from missing Vanshika. His love for her
remained, unwavering and constant, but he found himself
embracing a quiet acceptance that didn't rely on her return.
Instead, he let the memories shape his days, holding onto
them as gently as one might hold onto a precious, fragile
keepsake.

One evening, as Shivam sat alone in his room, he came
across an old photo they had taken together during one of
their outings. The image brought back a flood of emotions,
but instead of feeling the usual sting of loss, he felt a calm
nostalgia wash over him. They had shared something
beautiful, and though it was no longer a part of his present,
it would always remain a cherished chapter in his life.

As he looked at the photo, he whispered quietly, *"Vannu,
tum hamesha mere saath rahogi, chahe zindagi humein
alag raahon par le jaye."*

In that moment, he realized that his love for Vanshika had
grown into something beyond expectation. It was a quiet
devotion, a silent promise to carry her memory without
demanding anything in return. He understood that while he
would always wait for her in some corner of his heart, his
life had to move forward with or without her presence.

That night, he called Vasundhra to share his thoughts, his
voice calm and steady.

"Vasundhra," he said, *"main uska intezaar toh karta hoon,
par yeh intezaar ab us umeed ke bina hai jo kabhi kabhi*

*mujhe dard deti thi. Yeh bas ek khamoshi hai, jo mujhe uske
saath jod ke rakhti hai."*

Vasundhra's response was gentle and understanding.
*"Shivam, yeh tumhari pyaar ki khubsurti hai. Tumne usse
bina kisi shart ke apnaya hai, aur shayad yahi tumhare
pyaar ki asal taqat hai."*

Her words settled over him like a warm blanket, comforting
and reaffirming his feelings. Shivam had found a way to
hold onto his love without letting it hold him back. He
could wait for her, but his life would continue to grow,
grounded in the strength of their shared memories.

With a quiet sense of peace, he let himself close his eyes,
holding her memory close but without the weight of
longing.

As time continued to pass, Shivam's days grew softer around the edges, his memories of Vanshika becoming less like sharp pangs and more like gentle reminders of what they had shared. He carried on with his routines, allowing his love for her to live quietly within him, no longer needing to check his phone constantly or ask friends for updates.

One weekend, while visiting a bookstore, he came across a poetry collection that reminded him of the verses he had once written for her. Flipping through its pages, he felt a sense of kinship with the words—each line echoed his own journey, a tale of love that had blossomed and endured, even without a defined ending.

He bought the book and spent the rest of the evening at a nearby café, losing himself in its verses. Each poem seemed to capture a different part of his journey, and by the time he reached the final page, Shivam felt a new surge of clarity. His love for Vanshika wasn't tied to a future he could hope for but rather to a past that had shaped him, making him who he was now.

Later, he met up with Sujal and Vasundhra, sharing his thoughts openly as they sat together.

"You know," Shivam said, staring thoughtfully at his coffee, *"shayad woh mere saath nahi hai, par uske saath bitaye hue pal mere hamesha saath rahenge. Aur shayad yeh yaadein hi kaafi hain."*

Sujal gave a small nod, his expression understanding. *"Shivam, pyaar ka asal matlab wahi hai. It's about embracing what you shared, even if it's no longer in your life."*

Vasundhra added, her voice gentle. *"Tumne apne pyaar ko ek ehsaas banake apne saath rakh liya hai, Shivam. Shayad isi mein tumhari tasalli hai."*

In that moment, Shivam realized the depth of his own growth. He would always love Vanshika, but that love had become a quiet strength, not a burden. He didn't need to keep waiting in the same way; instead, he could let her memory walk beside him, guiding him without holding him back.

That night, Shivam wrote a final line in his notebook, one that captured his journey from longing to peace.

"Woh pal ab bhi mere hain, unmein woh muskuraati hai, Aur main uske intezaar mein, par uske bina jee bhi leta hoon."

With that, he closed the notebook, feeling a sense of closure—not an end to his love, but a new beginning in how he carried it.

Shivam found comfort in his quiet acceptance, carrying Vanshika's memory as a cherished part of himself rather than a source of unfulfilled hope. He allowed her absence to be a gentle presence in his life, a reminder of love that had once been real, deep, and transformative. The more he embraced this, the more he found peace.

One evening, as he walked through the city streets, he felt a familiar warmth settle over him, as if Vanshika's essence walked beside him. It wasn't an ache anymore; it was simply a feeling—a gentle reminder of everything they had shared. The love he held for her didn't feel unfinished but rather complete in a way he hadn't understood before.

When he returned home that night, he opened his notebook for what felt like the last entry about her, reflecting on the journey he'd been on since they'd parted.

"Woh meri zindagi ka hissa thi, aur rahegi,
Uske bina bhi uska ehsaas mere saath chalega."

With those words, Shivam closed the notebook, feeling a quiet fulfillment. Vanshika would always be part of him, but he no longer felt bound by the need to wait for her. Instead, he felt liberated, carrying her memory as a piece of himself rather than a weight to bear.

He took a deep breath, letting the silence settle around him, knowing that his love for her had transformed. It was no longer about whether she would return but about how her presence had shaped him, strengthened him, and left him with a heart capable of enduring.

The years stretched out before him, and though he would carry her memory, he knew he could walk forward with a lightness he hadn't felt in a long time. Shivam had found peace—not because he had moved on, but because he had found a way to live with his love, keeping it as a quiet strength.

"Kabhi kabhi, pyar ka matlab bas uske yaadon mein jeena hota hai,
Aur woh yaadein hi zindagi ko ek maayne de deti hain."

In that quiet realization, Shivam found closure—not as an end to his love but as a new beginning, a way to live fully with the memory of everything they had shared.

The Hope That Remains

As the days turned into months, and months into years, Shivam's life continued to unfold. He moved forward, finding new moments of joy, new friendships, and new experiences, but the love he held for Vanshika remained a quiet constant in his heart. Though he had learned to live fully, embracing each day with a renewed sense of purpose, there was a part of him that still held onto a hope only he understood.

In moments of stillness, Shivam would look back on everything they had shared, remembering her smile, her laughter, and the way her presence had lit up his world. And though life had led them down separate paths, he found comfort in the belief that someday, somehow, their paths might cross again.

He often whispered to himself, *"Kuch intezaar shayad hamesha ke liye hote hain, aur woh intezaar apne aap mein ek kahani ban jaate hain."*

It wasn't a desperate waiting but a gentle faith, a quiet belief that what was meant to be would find its way. Shivam's love for Vanshika had transformed into a silent strength, a reminder of the beauty of unbroken bonds, no matter how far apart life had taken them.

And so, he waited—not as someone bound by loss, but as someone who understood that love, once truly felt, could never really leave. His heart held onto the hope that one day, when the time was right, their story might begin anew.

Until then, he cherished the love he carried, knowing that even in waiting, he had found a strength few could understand.

"Woh aaye ya na aaye, par yeh dil uske intezaar mein hamesha zinda rahega."

And with that enduring hope, Shivam walked forward, his heart forever tied to the memory of the love that had changed him.